How Far Are You Willing To Go?
Murder Is Just The Beginning
(Rated PG)

How Far Are You Willing To Go?
Murder Is Just The Beginning
(Rated PG)

BY

TRACY WILSON

http://beautifulpublications.com

Published by
Beautiful Publications LLC
Stratford, CT 06614

PRINT ISBN: 978-0-9985765-0-3
EBOOK ISBN: 978-0-9985765-3-4

Printed in the United States of America

Dedication

This series is dedicated to my granddaughter, Shaliyah.

Thank You

To my family, friends, and fans for providing me with unconditional support, all your feedback, and for wanting more. This is for you too.

This was the 2ⁿᵈ time I won something from KISS FM! The first time I won something from KISS FM, I won a trip for two to see Luther Vandross and Nancy Wilson in concert at the Crystal Palace in Nassau, Bahamas. I went with my sister and I tried to cram everything I could into that weekend.

My sister doesn't usually drink but when she saw a liquor store with different flavored Bacardi and little sample cups, she couldn't resist trying at least one of them. 11 samples later, we were giggling and chatting with people in the store like we were in the club! It was a little after 11 a.m. – since we had finished our "liquor" breakfast we needed to look for a place to have lunch…but back to the prize I won this time…

I was the 19th caller and my prize was two tickets to Krystals – a club in Jamaica Queens. I was so excited I had to call my best friend Char (short for Charlotte). Char is always there when you need someone to talk to, hang out with, and, even if she's not hungry, if you want her to eat something so you're not eating by yourself, she'll eat again – especially if it's your treat! She'll cut you up in a second – and she can cut through you and break you down to tears with razor sharp words if she feels you need it, but she has a heart of gold and if she has a dollar and you need 50 cents, she'll break that dollar just to help you out.

The phone rang twice before she picked it up…

"Hello?" Char asked as she answered the phone.

"Do you know how to get to Krystals?"

"What's Krystals?"

"It's a club in Jamaica Queens."

"Why you wanna know if I know how to get there?"

"'Cause I just won two tickets from KISS FM for Friday night and I want you to go with me."

"Oh ok – if you find out how to get there, I'll go. Find out if we gotta dress up and let me know."

"Okay – talk to you later."

I called Krystals and asked for directions. I didn't mind that it would take us two hours by subway but I hoped Char wouldn't mind either. The way I saw it, two hours was worth it to get into Krystals for free – especially on Friday night – KISS FM was there live!

When I talked to Char later, she reminded me that it was more than two hours – a lot more – we had to walk from the train then stand outside for about an hour to get in because the line was so long. I didn't even think about how tired we would be when we left, our aching feet, the walk to the train, the ride on the train trying to stay awake, etc., but as luck would have it, after Char reminded me of all this, she still wanted to go! Whew!

When we got to Krystals, as expected, we had a while to wait online while they searched everyone. After about an hour, two gentlemen approached us with a clip board...

"Are you on tonight's guest list?"

"Yes we are – look under Trenice Robertson."

"We don't see you here – are you sure?"

Oh my God! I don't know what I was more afraid of – that we were about to be rejected from the club in front of all these people, or Char. She gave me that look – the one you get when someone's about to, "No-the-fuck-you-did-not-have-me-come down here, stand on line for over an hour," but she didn't! Whew!

In that instant, one of the gentlemen said, "Wait here - let me go check the other guest list...."

I was sure everyone could hear me praying out loud, "Lord, please let my name be on that list." Worst case scenario, I would have paid the $30 for us to get in – after 3 hours we were gettin' our groove and drink on!

"Miss Robertson, everything's ok – you and your guest can come on in."

I turned and looked back at the crowd with a 'yea-that's-right-I'm-on-the-list' smirk - you know damn well they were waitin' for us to be thrown off the line and out the club!

When it came to the search, I got uncomfortable with the quickness. They had a male bodyguard to search the men, and a female bodyguard to search the ladies. Normally this isn't a problem but after I saw how she was pattin' all over this woman in front of me, I knew she wasn't touchin' me...

"Excuse me. Please don't be offended, but I would feel better if he did the search."

She gave a look like, 'what-the-fuck,' but the male body guards smirked at me as if I was flirting with them both and before I could say anything else, one of them grabbed me by the arm, patted me down and said, "Next." Char didn't mind him pattin' her down either.

When we got inside, we looked around for the most important things: the bathroom, the fire exit, the main exit, the bar, and the men. We went into the bathroom and were cordial with the ladies we met in there.

After coming out, I told Char the first round was on me so I proceeded to the bar. After I ordered 2 Bacardi and Coke's, gave the bartender $20 and didn't get back any change, I informed Char that we wouldn't be doing too many rounds!

After we finished our drinks, Char found someone to dance with so I started looking for someone to dance with for myself. Everyone was either dancing with someone or more interested in holding up the wall than dancing so I went into the middle of the floor near Char and her friend and started dancing by myself. A few girls that were sitting at a table decided to get up and join me so I had plenty of company. I had worked up quite a sweat so I sat down to take a break. He sat down beside me.

"Hello."

"Hi." I figured no harm in being cordial.

"You enjoying yourself?"

"Yes."

"I saw you dancing earlier."

"You wanna dance?" I just assumed this is where he was leading but you know what happens when you assume right?

"No - I don't dance. I came with a friend of mine and he's dancing so I'm just gonna sit."

I shrugged my shoulders as if to say, "Oh well," and got up to go sit somewhere else.

"Where you goin'?"

This kinda surprised me 'cause I really didn't think he was the least bit interested but I didn't feel the need to be rude so I said, "I'm here with my best friend – I wanna see where she's at."

"Oh ok – come back when you find her."

"Ok I will. Hmm," I thought.

I found Char and pointed him out at the table so she would see where I was at. He was all smiles. I went back to the table and sat down.

"I didn't think you would come back."

"Well, you thought wrong I guess."

We both laughed then he got to the point...

"Are you seeing anyone right now?"

Usually I would say yes when this happened 'cause it was true or I wasn't interested and I didn't want to hurt the guy's feelings, but this time it wasn't either. My answer; however, was just as disappointing.

"No, but I'm pursuing someone right now."

"Pursuing someone?" He had a perplexed look on his face so I figured I might as well tell him the truth. I don't know why I felt so comfortable with him but the perplexed look on his face was so sad and familiar, I felt I had to explain. I wasn't sure what difference it would make, but I couldn't just leave it like that so I proceeded to tell him all about Tony...

"I met Tony after I moved in with my grandmother. I was coming into the building with my groceries and he held the door for me. That was unusual – usually the guys would hurry past you and let the door close in your face. After holding the door for me, he helped me with my groceries to my door – that's when I found out we were neighbors and he lived with his grandmother too.

Tony was different from other guys in the complex – he was kinda shy in a way. You never saw him drinking a forty outside, being loud like the rest of them. He would get his smoke on though, but if you were asleep, he didn't wake you up with loud-ass noise under your window. He was respectful to the ladies in the complex – he held door for them, helped them with their groceries, helped them with their carriages, and he would even offer to call you a taxi if you were waiting and cussin 'cause they told you 5 minutes and it had been 20 minutes. Whenever I saw him I would always say, "Hello Tony," and his friends would mock me in unison, "Hello Tony." This went on for two weeks. When I would see him outside alone, I would sit next to him and we would talk about our day at work, the weather, TV shows, etc, until his friends came along and said in unison, "Hello Tony." Sadly, he would get up and tell me, "Well, I guess I'll see you later," and he would go inside.

One night I saw Tony outside and I sat down to talk with him. We were having a good conversation and I was about to tell him how I felt about him but, like clockwork, here come his friends, mocking me in unison, "Hello Tony." When he got up to leave, I gently tugged his arm and said, "It's nice out and it's Friday night. Let's stay outside for a while." As happy as I was that he sat back down, I was so mad that his friends decided to sit down and join us. I was determined to tell him how I felt, even if it meant waiting all night until his friends went inside. After about ½ hour, his friends went inside and we were alone – finally!

"I really like you Tony."

"I really like you too Trenice."

"I was beginning to wonder about that – every time your friends came around, you left."

"I wanted to tell you how I felt, but I was afraid of what you would say."

"Tony, I need your help in the kitchen…."

"Shit!" I said to myself. "Just when we were gettin' somewhere…"

"Well, I better go inside, I'll see ya later."

"I'd seen Tony a couple of times since then and he would always say hello, hold the door for me, and help me with my groceries, but we haven't spoken about that night since."

I couldn't believe it. I had just spilled out my guts to a complete stranger. I don't know why I did or why he listened. Why did he listen? He gave me his undivided attention the whole time.

After a few minutes of silence he said, "Don't get me wrong, but hasn't he taken up enough of your time? He had his chance – he blew it – now it's my turn."

"Your turn?"

"Yes. I've seen you before and I wanted to talk to you but I thought you were involved. I couldn't believe my luck when I saw you in here tonight. When you pointed me out and came back to the table, I knew I had to talk to you tonight. Lets go someplace where we can talk some more. Why don't you tell your friend you're going with me? I'll make sure you get home."

Hold up! I wanted to go with him. It had been a long time since I enjoyed myself like this. I felt like I could talk with him forever. I trusted him. But Char and I had a rule: we go out together, we go home together. Period. As bad as I wanted to go with him, the other voice in my head started yelling at me...

"Are you crazy? You don't even know his name! You don't know anything about him!"

My other voice said, "There's something about him... you can trust him, this feels right..."

"Trenice I'm ready," Char said, interrupting my thoughts.

"Char this is...by the way, what is your name?"

"Jordan." I liked that...

"Char, Jordan has invited me to go with him and he'll make sure I get home."

Char's eyes popped out her head and she opened her mouth to cut me down, but I was one up on both of them – before she could say a word I said, "They take pictures right?"

"Why?" Jordan looked perplexed too – good!

"Well, he can take a picture of us and I'll give it to you. If you don't hear from me by tomorrow afternoon, you can give it to the police and tell them, "This is the person she left with."

Char's eyes got wide again, but she had a big smile on her face. She taught me well. Whenever she met someone she would call me and give me the digits, the address, and the license plate to the car. If I didn't hear from her within 24 hours, I was to call the police. She even told them, "My best friend has your digits, your address, and your license plate and if she doesn't hear from me in the morning, she's going to the police." Thank God I always heard from her.

Jordan smiled to himself and when we posed for the picture, he snuck up behind me, placed his arm around my waist, and gently pulled me close to him. "Take two," he said. The 1st picture he gave to Char. "You can give this back to Trenice later." The 2nd picture he put in his pocket.

"Can we drop Char off and then go where ever we're going?"

"Sure." We went outside to the car and got in.

"Do you have a driver's license?"

"Of course."

"May I see it?"

"Sure."

I took one look at his driver's license and bust out laughing. Jordan seemed annoyed but didn't say anything. I passed it to Char and she took one look at it and bust out laughing.

Jordan looked back at Char, looked at me, and said in a somewhat annoyed tone, "So where to Char?"

"Across the street from you."

We all bust out laughing.

Chapter 2

Jordan and I spent the wee hours of the morning at the movies! After leaving Yonkers, we drove all the way back to New York City and found an all night theatre on 42nd Street. They were running Star Wars, The Empire Strikes Back, and Return of the Jedi back to back for the price of 1 movie. I loved the Star Wars movies – this was great!

We got out the movies at 7 a.m. I was dead-tired, but I didn't want to go home. "I'm tired but I don't wanna go home yet."

"So let's not go home then." We went to IHOP for breakfast. I had pancakes with blueberries and Jordan had pancakes with strawberries. We also had fruit salad, scrambled eggs with cheese, turkey sausage, and coffee. It was 9 a.m. when we finally asked the waitress for the check. She seemed a bit annoyed but when Jordan gave her a $20 tip, she was happy indeed.

As we talked on the way home, I found out that Jordan's grandmother and my grandmother knew each other and they were good friends. My grandmother always talked about her good friend April but who'd a thought? I lived with my grandmother, Jordan lived with his grandmother, and they were good friends. Just when I started feeling really high on life, Jordan leaned over and kissed me on the cheek. When he got out and opened the door for me I thought, "Oh God – I hope were not related...."

"You slept with him didn't you?"

"No Grandma."

"Yes you did."

"No I didn't Grandma – I would tell you if I did."

And I would have too. Grandma was cool that way. She made us feel comfortable from early on – whatever we wanted to tell her we could. We had to be prepared for the consequences but she had our back and she believed it was better for us to come to her before something happened so she could prevent it. Whenever you went to Grandma she would call Mom and say, "What did you do to this child this time?" Whatever you told Grandma stayed with Grandma – or so I thought...

Chapter 3

It was 1 pm when I called Char. "Girl, I was comin' over there to tell Grandma. So how was it?"

"Char, he's wonderful! We went to the movies then breakfast. You know Grandma had to grill me when I came in right?"

"Well did you?"

"No."

Chapter 4

I called Jordan at 10 a.m. on Sunday. When I got off the phone at 2 p.m. Grandma said, "Whad ya do – tell him your life story? That's the longest you've ever been on the phone!"

I was on cloud 9 for the rest of the day. I couldn't believe we talked for so long – I don't even remember half of what we said – all I knew was I didn't want the conversation to end. His voice was soothing and comforting and I was beginning to realize that Jordan was giving me something that had been missing in my life for a long time. I enjoyed being alone but I was tired of being lonely. Besides, it had been 6 months since I broke things off for good with Torbett and I needed to move on. I needed everything Jordan could provide.

It had been 6 months since I broke it off with Torbett but it was over between us long before then. In the beginning of our relationship Torbett and I were inseparable. I had met him in my senior year of high school. Once I graduated from high school, Torbett and I moved in together. We lived together for about a year and things were fine until Torbett lost his job.

I was working but it wasn't enough. It didn't take long for Torbett to lose his temper. He would fly off the handle whenever he came in after 2 a.m. smelling like liquor and I asked where he was all day. Losing his job and his temper wasn't enough – that damn fool lost his mind when he slapped me for questioning him. I was smart enough to know that at 6 foot 10, 300 pounds he would break my ass in half if I slapped him back, but I was even smarter to leave his ass!

"Trenice, please don't leave – it'll never happen again..."

"I know that's right," I said as I walked out the door and headed straight to Grandma's house.

Grandma never liked Torbett. "There's something about him..." she always said. But she never butt in when Torbett came over and talked me into giving him another chance. Everything was ok for a while. Torbett had gotten himself a good job and he had cut down on the drinking considerably. We met each other on Fridays, we got a room for the weekend, and I was back at Grandma's house on Sunday night. After a month, Torbett started coming to pick me up every other weekend. It seems he was working overtime so he couldn't pick me up every weekend like before. After two months of this, it was once a month. That voice went off in my head, "What are you doing? You deserve a lot more than this."

I picked up the phone as Grandma was on her way into the kitchen to make coffee. "Hello? Torbett?"

"Yes?"

"It's over. If you have anything to say, don't bother. I don't want to hear it. Don't come by to see me. I have nothing else to say to you after this. If you send any letters, I'll return them unopened. First we were seeing each other once a week. Then twice a month. Then once a month. Now we're not seeing each other at all. Goodbye."

"Okay." Dial tone.

That was all he had to say. That told me I did the right thing. Grandma came out of the kitchen sipping her coffee. She looked at me and smiled without saying a word. I met Tony the following week and that brings us back to Jordan.

Chapter
5

Jordan came over to Grandma's house a week later to meet her. It was Father's Day, June 15th. Grandma liked him immediately. I listened intently as she told Jordan stories about how she was the bartender at the Black Horse, which Jordan's grandmother owned. She laughed and continued to talk about how she and his grandmother would help the bouncers throw people out of the bar when they had too much liquor and she and his grandmother would go clubin' together on their days off.

When Jordan asked if she ever met his father she said, "Yea, I knew him," then she changed the subject. "So where are you and Trenice off too?" I wondered why she did such an about face but I didn't worry about us being related anymore 'cause

Grandma would've told me from jump if she thought I had anything to worry about.

"We're going downtown to the movies and dinner." I already knew where we were going and I couldn't wait to leave and spend the day with him.

We spent the day in the city. We went to central park, the movies, and Tad's Steakhouse for dinner. When Jordan brought me home, Aunt Trudy was all in it...

"Hi Trenice – who's this?"

"Hi Aunt Trudy – this is Jordan."

"Where'd you meet?"

"We met at Krystals."

"How long y'all been going out?"

"Two weeks."

"Oh that's nice – alright Ma - I'll see you later – nice meeting you Jordan," she said as she left.

"Well I better get going – I gotta get up early for work tomorrow – let me say good night to your grandmother."

That was the highlight of my day! Torbett had never done that unless my grandmother was in the living room when we got home. "Grandma, can you come out here? Jordan wants to say good night." I guess that was the highlight of her day too 'cause she came out grinning from ear to ear.

"Good night Miss Gladys."

"Good night Jordan."

He gave me a kiss on the cheek and went out the door.

"Sit down and tell me about your day."

"Well Grandma, it was great..." I was interrupted by a knock on the door.

"Who?"

"Trudy."

I opened the door and let her in.

"Trenice was just gettin' ready to tell me about her date."

"Ma, he's married. His wife's name is Rosalind and I work with her at the hospital. I saw Jordan come take her to lunch the other day."

"Are you sure Trudy?"

"I'm sure Ma."

"Don't tell him I told you Trenice – just break it off now."

"Okay I will," I lied. "Oh no the hell he didn't," I thought to myself.

"All right Ma – I'll see ya later."

"All right Trudy." Soon as the door closed she asked, "What are you gonna do?"

"I'm gonna tell him what Aunt Trudy said tomorrow Grandma."

Jordan came to pick me up Monday night. I waited for him outside in front of the building purposely because I wanted to question him without my grandmother and Aunt Trudy in his face. He must have been running late because I had been waiting an hour already.

"You've been waiting a long time."

I turned around and who was standing there but Tony!

"Yea I have been." All I could think was, "Oh now you wanna talk to me," but I bit my lip.

"I would never keep you waiting this long." I wanted to tell him, "Mothafucka he's only kept me waiting an hour – you kept me waiting for a couple of weeks!" but I bit my lip again.

"I'm sure he's on his way."

"You look cold – here take my jacket."

"Thanks."

"I'll sit here and keep you company but if he's not here in another ½ hour, you should go back upstairs."

I wanted Jordan so bad just then. I just wanted to save face. I don't know why I cared what Tony thought but I did. Just as I started gettin' anxious Jordan came flying around the corner...

"Sorry I'm late – I had to help Grandma. You still wanna go? If you're mad I'll understand." Mad was the last thing I was.

"Thanks for the jacket Tony," I said as I gave it back to him.

"I'm Jordan – nice to meet you – good lookin' out," he said as he shook Tony's hand.

When we walked around the corner I stopped at a stoop and sat down. "We need to talk Jordan – sit down."

"What's wrong?"

"Remember when you came to Grandma's house and met my Aunt Trudy?"

"Yea."

"Well, she says you're married. She says your wife's name is Rosalind and she works at the hospital with her. She also said you came to pick her up for lunch one day last week."

I watched the expression on Jordan's face change. He was sad, but then he got quite angry. "Rosalind is my ex-wife. We got a divorce 6 months ago. I was at the hospital last week to drop off some papers. I was gonna tell you tonight. You still wanna go out?"

"Yea."

"Okay let's go then."

We went to the city, to central park, to the movies, and out to dinner. I had a good time but I could tell Jordan was preoccupied. That was understandable. We didn't talk much – we just walked hand in hand or arm in arm.

I decided to give him the benefit of the doubt and trust him. When he brought me back home Grandma had her own agenda.

"Sit down Jordan." Oh boy. Here it comes.

"Grandma, Jordan…"

"Shut up Trenice!" I sat down and shut up quick.

"I heard you were married – is that true?"

"Yes. Rosalind is my ex-wife. We've been divorced for 6 months. I told Trenice tonight."

"Well if you wanna see my granddaughter again, I better see some divorce papers. Good night."

Grandma beat me to the punch. I had every intention of asking to see those papers but she told me to shut up so I didn't open my mouth.

"Good night Miss Gladys." He kissed me on the cheek and closed the door behind him.

I didn't hear from Jordan for over a week. Grandma didn't say anything about it either. Thank God she didn't 'cause I don't know what I would have said.

The following Saturday there was a knock at the door. Grandma was in the kitchen making us coffee…

"Who?"

"Jordan." I was so happy I ran to the door, opened it, and went to throw my arms around him but he pushed me back.

"I need to see your grandmother."

"Come on in Jordan," she said as she sat our coffee on the table and I noticed Jordan was carrying a metal box. We sat at the table and Jordan pulled up a chair and scooted between Grandma and me.

"I have something to show you Miss Gladys," he said as he pulled out a bunch of papers and spread them out on the table. Grandma went over each paper as if it were a contract she had to sign. Jordan had a very serious look on his face. I was so happy I wanted to cry, but I fought back tears. Jordan sat back and watched as Grandma went through the divorce papers.

"Ok Jordan, you can put these away now."

"So I have permission to see your granddaughter?"

"You have my permission," she said.

Jordan went to pick up all of the papers to put them back in the metal box but I snatched them up before he could. I turned to the last page. The divorce was granted about 6 ½ months ago.

Tuesday night Aunt Trudy came over again. "Hi Ma, hi Trenice. What happened with you and Jordan?"

"Oh we're fine."

"But I told you he was married."

"But I saw his divorce papers," Grandma yelled from her bedroom.

I heard a knock on the door, but Aunt Trudy beat me to it..."Hi Jordan," she said slyly as she opened the door.

I was waiting for him to say, "Don't fuckin' speak to me," but instead he said, "Hello Trudy – Trenice you ready?"

"Yea."

"See you later Trudy – bye Miss Gladys."

"Bye Jordan," Grandma yelled from her room.

When we got out into the hallway, Jordan kissed me on the lips for the first time. Finally!

"I love you," he said as he pulled me in close to him.

"We better get going before someone comes into the hallway," I said between kisses...

"Yea we better," he said as we continued kissing for a few minutes. As bad as I wanted him we had a lot more to talk about before I took that step.

Chapter 7

I knew after the movies and dinner we would need to talk. I had planned to wait until tomorrow but Jordan wasn't waiting until then. To tell the truth, neither was I.

We were at Tad's Steakhouse and we had already ordered. We had a cozy table in the corner in the back. The lights were dimmed so it looked like we were eating by candlelight. "It's now or never," I thought...

"So how'd you like it?" Jordan asked as he interrupted my thoughts.

"The movie? Oh it was good..." I knew damn well he wasn't talking about the movie.

He smiled at me and said, "How'd you like the kiss?"

"Oh that." I leaned across the table, pulled his face to mine and kissed him.

"Ahem!" We both looked up and there was the waiter with our steaks and salads. "Will there be anything else?"

"Not right now, but if we change our mind, we'll call you," I said.

"That was nice," Jordan said.

"Yes it was – but we need to talk."

"What's wrong?"

"Nothing – nothing at all but..."

"Are you sure everything's ok?"

"Let me finish."

"Ok."

"Before I met Torbett I was in a relationship with Nathaniel. I really loved him and I thought he really loved me too. He used to tell me I was his number 1 lady. One day his twin brother, Daniel, sat me down to explain what that meant. Nathaniel did love me and I was his number 1 lady – but Chelly was number 2, Tonya was number 3, Vicki was number 4 etc. I couldn't deal with that. If this is a problem for you or if you're seeing other people let me know right now so we can go our separate ways."

I waited for Jordan to say something but he didn't. He just looked at me for about a minute without blinking.

"Are you ok?"

"Yea – it's just that I've never been told that before." He then proceeded to tell me about his ex-wife.

"I really loved Rosalind. We were married two years after we met. I really loved her. Even after I found out she was seeing someone else while we were married, I stayed with her for a while to try and work it out. When she told me she was pregnant I was ecstatic but she told me she wasn't ready for a baby. She had an abortion without telling me. That really hurt but I stayed with her for a while anyway. I just couldn't let go until she gave me no choice. When she got pregnant the 2nd time she put the knife in my back and twisted it. She told me it was Steven's baby and she wanted to end our marriage and be with him."

I saw tears in Jordan's eyes for the first time. I took his left hand and placed it gently in mine. The waiter came over and when he saw the tears in Jordan's eyes he turned and walked away.

We didn't say anything else while we finished our dinner. We walked to the subway hand in hand or arm in arm. The whole ride home we just sat next to each other holding each other. When we got home he kissed me passionately. "I love you. Good night."

I stood at the door and watched him walk downstairs.

I couldn't sleep. It was 2 a.m. Wednesday morning. I heard Grandma put the chain on the door like she always does once she knows I'm in for the night. As she walked down the hallway I smelled her coffee and I wanted some so I got up and made myself a cup. I sat at the kitchen table and wrote Jordan this poem:

I Can't Believe I'm In Love

You changed my life when you came in my world,
Now I'm glad that I'm your girl.
I Can't Believe – I Can't Believe I'm In Love.

Lonely my sickness – you're my cure.
I want this feeling forever more.
I Can't Believe – I Can't Believe I'm In Love.

Deep inside I know it's not infatuation.
When you hold me tight I can feel good vibrations.
I just want you to be mine until the end of time

God has answered my every prayer.
He sent someone who really cares.
I Can't Believe – I Can't Believe I'm In Love.

Chapter 8

I was dead tired. It was 3 p.m. and I was comin' down. Good thing I had a lot to do 'cause I'd be asleep at this desk. All I could think about was stopping by Jordan's house after work. I was nervous about giving him the poem I wrote. What would he think of it? Would he like it? Would he think I was silly? Would he think I was immature? 4:45 p.m. – shit I gotta go! I punched out and ran to Jordan's house.

When I got there I knocked on the door. "May I help you?"

"I'm Trenice – is Jordan home?"

"He's not here – you wanna wait for him?"

"Sure."

"You look familiar – what's your mother's name?"

"Claire."

"Claire's your mother? You look just like her! I've known your mother and grandmother for years!"

"You're Miss April?" I asked.

"Yes – I'm Jordan's grandmother and this is his mother, June."

"Nice meeting you both." Just then, Jordan came in the door.

"Hey Mum-Mum – hey Trenice – whatchu doin' here?"

"I have something for you."

Let me change and then we can go outside." This took all but two minutes.

When we got downstairs, we saw Char. "Hi Trenice, hi Jordan!" she yelled as she drove past.

"So what you got for me?" he asked.

"Let's go somewhere and sit down." I said.

We walked to the park in the next block and found a bench off by itself. We sat down and I handed him my poem. He read the poem, put it back in his pocket and said, "It's nice." He took my hand and led me to the tree in the middle of the grass. When we sat down he slid up behind me, wrapped his arm around me and pulled me close to him. We stayed like that in the park and I fell asleep. Jordan woke me up at 8 p.m. and said, "I think I better get you home."

I got up Thursday morning and got ready for work as usual, but I was unusually quiet.

"What's your problem?" Grandma said.

"Nothing."

"Don't give me that nothing shit – what's wrong?"

"Nothing Grandma – really."

"Let me see your eyes...they mighty red – you been smoking that shit?"

"No Grandma – I'm just tired. There's nothing wrong – I swear."

"Well you better not be smoking that shit!"

"Grandma – you know I can't lie to you," I laughed. I was telling the truth on both counts. I wasn't smoking that shit and you couldn't lie to Grandma. She could see right through you - so don't even try it.

She smiled at me and said, "I know you don't lie to me."

"Have a good day," I said as I kissed her cheek and went off to work.

I got off work at 5 p.m. and Jordan was there waiting for me. "Let's go," he said as he took my hand.

"Where we goin'?" I asked as he pulled me across the street.

"Come with me," he said.

We went back to the park and sat down on the bench. Jordan took out a radio cassette player and popped in a tape. I cried as I listened to him singing to me the poem I wrote to him, which he put to his music. We went to a studio that weekend, had a demo made, and had our song copy-written.

The following week I was at Jordan's house every night after work. Miss June would stay in the bedroom and Miss April would come back and forth listening to us singing to the music we were playin' and listen to us singing to music we were makin'. Sometimes we got carried away and she'd yell, "People tryin' to sleep and it's gettin' late!" That was usually are cue to pack it in.

I remember the first time I sang for Jordan. I was nervous as hell. I had been singing in church and in chorus but I was afraid Jordan would tell me I couldn't sing. Nothing was further from the truth. Once he heard me sing he wanted me to sing all the time.

We spent every night at his house putting songs to music. Jordan was really impressed with my songs and my writing ability. He would often make comments like, "great analogy," or "nice change." I heard many of his songs and I picked out my favorites. In fact, my brother Marlowe would come downstairs (my mother, brothers, and sisters lived upstairs on the 4th floor and Jordan, his mother, and his grandmother lived on the 2nd floor) and he couldn't remember the name of the song he liked that Jordan wrote but he would ask, "Can I hear that song again?" The song was, 'Foolish Guy' and Jordan was always happy to play it for him.

I loved Jordan's voice too. I found out that he had been in a band in the 70's, 'Heat, Energy, & Mass' but the name was quickly changed to 'Stone.' Thomas Blidge, Mary J. Blidge's father, was the bass player and Jimmy Miller, Mary J. Blidge's uncle, was the guitar player. Jordan was nicknamed 'Gino-Smokey Robinson' because his voice was very similar to Smokey Robinson's voice. Jordan also performed Smokey Robinson's song, 'Tell Me Tomorrow' at Trevor Park in Yonkers every year when they had the African American Heritage Festival.

We also spent a lot of weekends at Cain's house in School Street where we sang with Arnette, DMX's mother. When I met William, the first thing I noticed was his strong resemblance to Lionel Richie. William had a voice that was better than Lionel Richie's — he could sing Lionel's songs but he could also hit notes higher than Philip Bailey, the lead singer of Earth, Wind, & Fire. William was also a songwriter and Jordan arranged his music on the song, 'Tonight,' and he co-wrote a song with William entitled, 'Never Thought.' I loved to hear William and Jordan sing together and whenever they needed a background singer, I was more than happy to volunteer.

Chapter 9

Jordan came to pick me up at 12 p.m. Saturday. I was wondering who was with him. When he came on the porch he introduced us.

"Jake, this is Trenice – Trenice, this is my best friend Jake and his lady Rachel. They're gonna chill with us today – do you mind?"

"No – I don't mind." To be honest I wasn't sure but what was I gonna say?

We went to the bus stop and caught the bus to the subway. We laughed and talked on the subway and got to know each other. Jordan seemed really happy that we got along so well.

We went to central park, the movies, and dinner. Before we left the restaurant, Rachel and I got up to go to the ladies room.

"So you like Jordan?" she asked me as she was fixin' her hair.

"Like him? I don't just like him – I love him." That was the first time I told anyone other than Jordan that I loved him.

We went back to the table and had dessert. After dessert we left the restaurant and went back to central park. We watched the sun go down and once it started to get chilly Rachel said, "Jake I'm ready to go."

"Why we gotta leave so soon?" Jake asked her.

"Cause I'm ready," she said in a seductive voice."

Jordan and I looked at them and then at each other. We were 'ready' too.

Chapter 10

Early Sunday morning Jordan came to pick me up for breakfast. I was waiting downstairs so I wouldn't wake up anyone in the house. There were only a few people out and I loved the peace and quiet. Jordan come up on the porch and kissed me hello. We went to the bus stop and once we were on the bus I was deep in thought.

"Why you so quiet?"

"Just thinking."

"Something good I hope?"

"Very."

We rode the subway to 42nd Street and went straight for breakfast. We went back to IHOP and started out with coffee and juice, then graduated to fruit, cheddar omelets, corn muffins, turkey sausage then refills on the coffee.

When we got home I had to call Char.
"Hello?"
"I'm comin' over," I said.
"Ok – I'll meet you downstairs."

Chapter 11

Jordan and I made an appointment for the following Monday. We agreed we would use the same doctor and that we would both be in the room when the doctor read us our results.

The doctor was pleasantly surprised. "I wish more of my patients did what you two are doing. It would save them all so much grief."

We were both given clean bills of health as far as the GYN exams, but we were told we would receive the results of the blood test in the mail in about two weeks.

I smiled to myself as we left the doctor's office.

Chapter 12

    I had been takin these fuckin' pills for two weeks and I was already sick of 'em — literally…"Ugh!"

    "What's wrong with you girl?"

    "Nothing Grandma — I'm just nauseous."

    "What you got the flu?"

    "I hope not Grandma."   When I came out the bathroom she corned me.

    "What's going on Trenice?"

    "Nothing Grandma."

    "Come sit down."   Oh boy — here it comes…

    "You want some coffee Trenice?"

    "Yea Grandma — sit down — I'll make it."   I figured I might as well tell Grandma 'cause she was gonna push the issue anyway. I put two cups of coffee on the table and sat down.

"You love him don't you?"

"Yes Grandma – very much."

"Your Aunt Trudy says you're pregnant. She saw you runnin' to the bathroom the other day. Are you?"

"No Grandma."

"You sure? Don't let me find out you lyin' to me..."

"Grandma you know I never lie to you."

"I know you never lie to me but I also know you're keeping something from me. Don't do like my daughters did – they told me after they were 5 months pregnant so I couldn't do anything about it. If you're pregnant just tell me – you know I love you no matter what and you also know you ain't ready for no baby."

I love my grandmother but I didn't want to tell her. Aunt Trudy had already seen me running to the bathroom. They probably talked about me and if Aunt Trudy asked her, she would tell her and Aunt Trudy has a big fuckin' mouth – I don't need the United States knowing my business. But I saw how Grandma was looking at me. I knew she loved me and I didn't want to hurt her – and I could see this was hurting her so I figured what the hell...

"Grandma?"

"Yes?"

"You know I been sick..."

"Yea? So?"

"It's from the pill."

"What pill?" I almost didn't want to answer her 'cause she had that 'bitch-don't-make-me-slap-you look on her face.

"Birth control pills. I'm on birth control Grandma." I waited for the 'you aint married lecture' but instead I got a big hug.

"Thank God you had the good sense to realize you ain't ready for no baby."

"I know Grandma. Me and Jordan went to the doctor last month to get checked and for me to start the pill."

"Hold it – get checked? He got something?"

"No Grandma – we just went together – I went for him and he went for me."

"Well you need to go back to the doctor and change those pills – you shouldn't be sick like that. If you had told me sooner I would have told you."

I went to the doctor and told her about my 'morning, noon, and night sickness.' She changed my prescription and I took them in the evenings instead of the morning. As usual, Grandma knew what she was talking about.

When I got back home I ran smack into Sissy – Aunt Trudy's girlfriend. I can't stand that nosy bitch.

"Are you or ain't ya?" she yelled to the whole fuckin' neighborhood. I kept walking like I didn't hear her. Fuckin' nosy bitch!

Chapter 13

I got my blood test results in the mail on Monday. I knew they would be negative but I opened them and read them anyway. "Negative," I said. Just like I thought. Just then I got a wonderful idea.

I called the Holiday Inn Crowne Plaza in White Plains. "Holiday Inn may I help you?"

"I'd like to book a room for Sunday night."

"Single?"

"Yes single."

"What credit card would you like to use?" "MasterCard."

I booked the room at the Holiday Inn Crowne Plaza in White Plains 'cause I didn't want to run into anybody in Yonkers – especially if I was going to a hotel with Jordan. I was so excited I ran to the bathroom to shower and get dressed…

I came out the bathroom smiling like the cat that swallowed the canary. I got dressed, went downstairs, and high-tailed it to Jordan's job. When I saw him I went flyin' across the store...

"Something wrong?"

"I got it."

"What?"

"The test results – did you get yours?"

"Wait here." I saw him go talk to someone – I guess it was his supervisor. "C'mon let's go home and check my mail."

We flew out the store to his house.

"Hi Mum-Mum did I get any mail?"

"Here – Hi Trenice."

"Hi Miss April – Hi Miss June."

"Jordan smiled to himself as he read the results then passed me the paper so I could read them. I read the results, took out my paper and gave it to him so he could read mine. He read the results, pulled me close and kissed me.

"I better get back to work..."

"Yea you better."

"Bye Mum-Mum."

"Bye Miss April – bye Miss June."

While we were walking back to his Job I told Jordan I had booked a room for Sunday at the Holiday Inn Crowne Plaza in White Plains. "See you Sunday," he said as he gave me a kiss.

"See you Sunday," I said as I headed back towards Grandma's house.

The next couple of days couldn't go by fast enough.

I got up Saturday morning and went to the bathroom. "Shit!" I yelled.

"You bang your toe again Trenice?"

"Yes Grandma."

"You need glasses Trenice? The toilet's so big – how can you miss it?"

"I guess so Grandma... Woo hoo!" I yelled.

"Trenice did you hit your damn toe again?"

"No Grandma – the water's cold – I'm in the shower!"

"Oh alright."

Chapter 14

"Hi Miss Gladys."

"Hi Jordan – where y'all goin' tonight?"

"Oh the usual – central park, the movies, dinner, walk around, chill."

"Well, don't have me sittin' up all night if you not comin' back tonight – let me know so I can put the chain on the door."

"Ok Grandma – we'll see ya later."

When we got downstairs Jordan asked, "Does she know?"

"Yea she knows."

We spent the majority of the morning in central park. Check in was 2p.m. so we had to find something to do until then. We figured we'd eat after we checked in. We rode the shuttle to Grand Central then took Metro North to White Plains.

When we got to White Plains it was 2 p.m. so we took a cab to the Holiday Inn Crowne Plaza. I presented my credit card and we went to the room. Once we got inside the door we looked around and we were in awe. A crystal chandelier hung from the ceiling in addition to the ceiling being mirrored. Plush peach carpeting soothed our aching feet and beige and gold furniture complimented the peach walls and carpet. There was a satin peach love seat on the left side of the room and a queen size bed on the right. A refrigerator was on the right side of the bed and the wall was mirrored behind the bed. To the left of the bed was the bathroom. The bathroom was peach, beige and gold with a Jacuzzi for two. Once we were ready for bed, we snuggled in under the covers... "Oh shit...Agghh!!!"

When I woke up I was in a hospital bed. I lay there for a minute and tried to get my bearings. "Oh God my head hurts. What's wrong with my foot? What happened?!" I screamed as tears came to my eyes...

Jordan, Jake, Rachel, Char, Aunt Trudy, Miss April, Miss June, Grandma, and my mother all burst into the room..."Don't cry baby its ok," Grandma said as everyone stood around.

"Mom?"

"I'm here baby – it's ok."

"Where's Jordan? What happened? Why am I here?!" I screamed as more tears came down my face.

"Calm down Trenice – it's ok," Jordan said as he came into the room and hugged me.

"Well, at least I know he didn't hurt me," I thought... "Or did he?"

"Hi Trenice – I'm Dr. Campton. You had quite a night huh? We're gonna keep you here overnight for observation because you have a mild concussion."

"Concussion? Doctor what's going on? Why is my foot in a cast? Why is my head bandaged up? Will somebody please answer me?!" I screamed as I started to cry again.

"You mean they didn't tell you? Well what are you all waiting for?" Dr. Campton asked.

"Honey we think Jordan should tell you," my mother said.

I looked at Jordan and I looked at everyone else in the room. No one seemed upset with him so I said, "Can you give us some privacy?" Everyone went into the hallway but Jordan. "Jordan I'm scared – please tell me what's going on," I said as I was crying.

"Don't cry Trenice – its ok," Jordan said as he kissed my head, my eyes, my nose, and my mouth. "I'm sorry."

I had to make sure I heard right. "What did you say?"

"I'm sorry."

Now I was mad. "What the fuck did you do to me?!" I screamed.

"Calm down it wasn't my fault – I swear!"

"Then why are you sorry?"

"Let me explain."

"Okay." I figured if his family and friends and my family and friends were outside and he wasn't in jail, then he must be telling the truth.

"Ok – remember when we were in bed?"

"How could I forget?"

"The frame on the bed broke, the bed hit the floor, your leg and foot got caught between the bed and the dresser, the lamp fell on your head, cut you, and you were unconscious."

"Oh my God!"

"I was so scared I didn't know what to do so I called an ambulance and the paramedics dressed you and brought you here. When they asked me who your next-next-of-kin was I told them to call your grandmother. I told her you were in an accident and she called your mother, Trudy, and Char. I called my Mum-Mums, Jake, and Rachel. I was so scared Trenice." He started to cry.

I was quiet for a moment then I bust out laughing. I was laughing so hard I was holding my stomach.

"What the fuck are you laughing at?!" He yelled.

"This whole thing! Who the fuck's gonna believe this shit?!" We were both laughing so hard everyone came into the room.

"Everything alright Trenice?" my mother asked.

"Yes – everything's fine," I laughed.

"Visiting hours are over – everyone's gotta go," the nurse interrupted.

"Ok – hugs everyone," I said. One at a time I got my hugs and kisses from everyone.

Chapter 16

It was Tuesday afternoon. Shit! There goes that nosy fuckin' bitch...Oh God – here she comes...

"You alright Trenice?"

"Yes Sissy – I'm ok."

"I heard what happened · damn girl he really laid you out huh?" Everyone around was laughing. Jordan cut his eyes at her like he wanted to knock the shit out of her.

"Excuse me · I need to get her in the house."

Sissy cut her eyes back at Jordan but she moved out the way so Jordan could wheel me into the building.

"Damn Trenice – you alright?" Tony asked.

"She's Fine!" Jordan growled. He bounced the wheel chair up the stairs and Tony went out the door without saying a word.

"Hi Miss Gladys."

"Hi Jordan – come on in – wait a minute – let me move the couch," she said as she pulled the couch away from the wall some. My mother and Aunt Trudy were there too.

"Honey help me up outta this wheelchair."

"You don't need to be on that foot Trenice," my grandmother said.

"I know Grandma but I can hop – and I gotta pee." They all hollered as I hopped down the hall.

I had to push myself on the back of the toilet and extend my leg so I could pee. I hit my broke foot on the tub…"Aagghh!!" I couldn't stop the stampede from comin' down the hall…the door burst open and there they stood: Grandma, my mother, Jordan, and Aunt Trudy. My pants were down around my ankles.

"Sorry – we just wanted to make sure you were ok," my mother said.

"Jordan can you help me please?"

"That's how you got in this mess in the first place Trenice – hasn't he help you enough?" My mother and Aunt Trudy laughed along with my grandmother.

"Oh I'm never gonna live this down am I Trenice?" Jordan asked.

"You? I live here – what about me?"

Jordan pulled my panties up to my waist, stood me up, pulled up my pants, and I leaned on him as I hobbled down the hall.

"I gotta get going – I'll come check on ya later. "By Miss Gladys – bye Trudy – bye Miss…Trenice what's your Mother's name?"

"Claire."

"Bye Miss Claire." He kissed me then went out the door.

"Alright Ma – we gonna go too," my mother said.

"Alright Claire, Trudy – see ya tomorrow."

"Trenice you call me if you need anything."

"I will Ma."

When they closed the door behind them I tried to hop into the kitchen but I tripped and hit the wall.

"Dammit Trenice - will you sit your ass down before you break your other damn foot!" my grandmother yelled.

"Ok Grandma – I'm sitting." I sat down for a minute and got back up – this time I put the pressure on my left foot and I used the rubber heel on my right foot.

"Trenice are you in the fridge?"

"Yes Grandma."

"Bring me a soda."

On Wednesday I went to see Char. It had been a week and ½ since I left the hospital and I was hobbling around pretty well. Char sat there with her mouth open and her eyes wide while I gave her all the details.

"Well girl you know that man I been seeing?"

"Yea Char I remember." I said. I loved Char but I hated that she only dated married men. Just last week she was telling me that she was tired of seeing married men and she wanted her own man. "I thought you were breaking it off with him?"

"I was girl."

"Char I don't want you to get hurt – what if his wife finds out?"

"Oh she won't but don't worry – I'm not tryin' to wind up dead – I don't go to his house or his job – he comes here."

"Well be careful girl."

"I will Trenice. I wish he'd leave his wife. He told me he wants to but he can't 'cause it will cost him too much and he'll lose everything."

"Char don't let him get away with that. He could string you along for years. You deserve better."

"Oh so now you know what's best for me 'cause you finally got a man? That makes you an expert? Who the fuck do you think you are?"

"Bye Char," I said as I got up from the kitchen table and went out the front door.

"Bye!" she yelled as I closed it. Sigh.

Chapter 18

It had been 3 weeks since I left the hospital. Jordan came by every night to see me and make sure I was ok. Sissy hasn't said another word to me since that day outside.

"Jordan what'd you say to Sissy?" Aunt Trudy asked.

"I didn't say shit to her!" This was only the 2nd time I had heard Jordan raise his voice.

"I just asked – don't bite my head off!"

"And I just told you."

"Le'me go Ma – see you later," she said as she slammed the door behind her.

"Bye Trudy," Jordan said as he kissed me hello. "How are you sweetheart?" he asked.

"I'm ok now that you're here but there's something I gotta do."

"What's that?" he asked as he watched me pick up the phone...

"Tyler Marshall Law Offices may I help you?"

"Yes – I'd like to make an appointment."

"How's next Monday at 10 a.m.?"

"Monday's fine."

"Your name?"

"Trenice Robertson."

"Can you give me a few details?"

"I'm filing suit against the Holiday Inn Crowne Plaza."

"Can you be more specific?"

"Not at this time."

"Ok Ms. Robertson I'll see you next Monday."

"Thank you."

"Are you serious?" Jordan asked.

"Damn right – I could'a broke my back."

"I hear you. Oh – before I forget – Jake and Rachel want us to hang out with them this weekend – you up for that?"

"I'm not sure I can be on my foot that long honey."

"We won't go far."

"Okay – long as we don't go too far." I didn't see Jordan again until the weekend.

Jordan came to pick me up – literally. "I'm goin' now Grandma."

"Alright – be careful."

"Ok I will Grandma."

"Bye Miss Gladys," Jordan said.

"Jordan?"

"Yes Miss Gladys?"

"Stay away from the Holiday Inn," she laughed.

We just looked at each other, then he picked me up and he carried me down the stairs.

"How you doin' Trenice – how's your foot?" Jake asked.

"I'm ok but I'd be better if people would stop with the jokes. My grandmother just HAD TO tell us to stay away from the Holiday Inn," I said as we all bust out laughing.

"That's why I'm suing their ass."

"You are?" Jake and Rachel asked.

"Hell yea – I could'a broke my back!"

"I hear that – they tried to break your back now break that bank," Rachel said as we all laughed again.

"I got me a good -ass lawyer too – Tyler Marshall & Associates. They specialize in personal injury and I didn't have to give them a retainer."

"I hear you girl," Rachel said.

We went to Tads for dinner, as usual, and laughed and talked for hours. The waiter didn't mind 'cause we kept eatin' and gettin' refills on iced tea so he knew he would be gettin' a nice tip. After dessert, we all got up to go back to the car. We drove to central park and sat there until the stars came out. Then, we all got in the car and Jake drove us home. When we got to Yonkers I asked, "Jake can you drop Jordan and I off at the park?"

"Sure."

"Trenice I gotta get up for work tomorrow – can it wait?" Jordan asked.

"I guess," I sighed.

"C'mon we'll go to the park."

"Ok – thanks Jake," I said.

"You're welcome Trenice – good night."

"Good night."

When we were alone in the park Jordan just sat their quiet.

"Let me get you home so I can get up for work tomorrow."

"Ok – let's go."

We smiled at each other as he picked me up, carried me down the stairs, and put me in the cab. When we got home he carried me upstairs and Sissy was in the hallway.

"Hi Sissy," I sneered. Sissy went into her apartment and slammed the door as Jordan put me down. Grandma was in the kitchen making herself a cup of coffee when I came in. "You gonna get that cast off soon huh Trenice?"

"Yep."

"You gonna stay away from that damn Holiday Inn?" she laughed.

"Good night Grandma," I said as I ignored her question.

"Good night Trenice," she said as she went down the hall to her bedroom.

I got to the lawyer's office at 9:30 a.m. The receptionist greeted me. "Ms.Robertson you're early. Would you like some coffee while you wait?"

"Yes please."

"You sure you don't wanna tell me what this is about?"

"You'll find out soon enough," I said with a laugh.

"It must be a doozy."

"You don't know the half of it," I said as I sat down and drank my coffee. Just as I was finishing my coffee Tyler came out into the lobby.

"Ms.Robertson I'm Mr. Marshall – please come into my office."

"Please call me Trenice," I said as I went into his office and closed the door.

"Very well, you can call me Tyler. Now what's this - I see you want to sue the Holiday Inn Crowne Plaza for $1,000,000?? What the hell did they do to you?"

Everyone in the office was standing outside the door when I opened it an hour later. Tyler couldn't control his laughter and neither could I. We looked around the office, looked at each other, and laughed some more.

"Ms. Robertson please tell me what's going on – you seem mighty happy for someone filling a million dollar law suit!" the receptionist said.

"Tyler will fill you all in I'm sure," I laughed.

"Trenice make sure your boyfriend comes to see me ASAP!"

"I will Tyler – and thank you for taking the case."

"Oh I wouldn't miss this for the world!" he said as I left the building.

The cab was waiting for me when I got downstairs. I got my first disability check for $250 but that would be gone in a minute by the time I paid for cabs back and forth to the law office in White Plains, the hospital, and back to Yonkers. After I left the hospital, I had the cab take me to Getty Square and wait.

"I charge extra for waiting miss."

"You'll get your money don't worry."

"You give me $40 now or I leave." He was charging me $40 for the trip from the law office, then to the hospital, the wait at the hospital, then the trip to Yonkers. "Ok here," I said as I handed him a $100 bill.

"Ok you go and I wait," he said.

"Ok you give me my $60 change then I go," I said. This motherfucker wasn't running out on me with my $100 – I ain't that fuckin' stupid!

"Here," he said as he threw three $20 bills at me.

"Never mind, you can go now – I'll get another cab," I said as I picked up the $20 bills, got out the cab, and slammed the fuckin' door. That jackass blew a $20 tip. Oh well, his loss.

I went through the store and smiled when I saw Jordan.

"What are you doing here?" he asked.

"You go to lunch yet?"

"No why?"

"Let's go – I got a lot to tell ya."

"Ok – yo John – I'm out – I'll be back at 2," he yelled.

"Alright Jordan – see ya later."

As we went through the store, one of Jordan's associates held the door for us so we could walk out. Jordan went to get the cab and I waited in the foyer. His associate approached me.

"Trenice can I ask you something?"

"Sure."

"What's he got that I haven't got?"

"Me," I said as Jordan came back to escort me to the cab.

"What was that about?"

"You," I said as I got in the cab. Jordan smiled as he went around and got in on the other side. We went to the Parkside Dinner for lunch. While we were waiting for our order I gave Jordan the 411.

"Are you serious?"

"Hell yea I'm serious."

"But I didn't get hurt."

"The hell you didn't."

"What do you mean?"

"When I got hurt in that hotel, you were scared to death. You were emotionally traumatized. Jordan sat there with his mouth wide open. He stared at me in disbelief. "You're right. I never thought about it that way. And I was scared."

"Exactly."

"I'll contact Tyler Marshall right away."

"Good."

We finished lunch and Jordan helped me to the cab he had waiting outside for us. He kissed me good bye and I had the cab drop me off at Char's house.

It had been almost 3 weeks since I'd seen Char. Char wasn't home so I waited outside for about 30 minutes. I missed my best friend. I wanted to apologize to her for upsetting her and I wanted my best friend back. I wanted to share my good news. My happiness was short-lived when she drove up with the married man.

"Watchu doin' here?!"

"I miss my friend."

"I miss my friend too," she said as she helped me up and we hugged.

"I'm sorry," we said to each other with tears in our eyes. We went upstairs and sat in the kitchen.

"I was mad at you because you were right Trenice."

"I just want you to have someone who loves you and only you. You're so special and you shouldn't have to hide and sneak around."

"We don't sneak around anymore girl," she said with a smile.

"Oh my God what happened? Details girl – details!"

"Well I thought about what you said and I told him I was tired of sneaking around - I wanted to be out in the open and have a real relationship."

"What'd he say?"

"He showed me separation papers girl!"

"Stop it! Really?"

"Yup. He got a legal separation from his wife. The divorce will be final in about 6 months. You know that bitch ain't letting go without a fight."

"I'm so happy for you Char. Looks like we both hit the jackpot."

"Girl, Jordan is the best thing that's happened to you in a long time."

"Yes he is – oh I forgot to tell you what's goin' on now..."

"What Trenice? Ya'll gettin' married?"

"I wish – but let me tell ya."

"Ok – what?"

"We're suing the Holiday Inn Crowne Plaza for $1,000,000!"

"Girl, you ain't gonna git that money."

"Oh we'll get some money alright. They'll be happy to settle when I get through with them."

"I hate to burst your bubble Trenice, but you ain't gettin' no real money. They'll probably just give you a couple thousand and pay your medical bills."

"Not when Tyler Marshall & Associates gets through with their ass."

"Tyler Marshall? How the fuck can you afford him?"

"That's the best part – personal injury doesn't require a retainer – they get paid when you get paid."

"Girl you go – let me know what happens."

When I got home I told Grandma about the law suit.

"Good – you should sue their ass – I don't know how much money you gonna get though."

"What money?" I turned around and there was Aunt Trudy and her nosy bitch ass friend Sissy. Just what the fuck I needed.

"I'm suing the hotel."

"Good – sue 'em then we can get paid."

"We?"

"Yea – I know you gonna share with family."

"No the fuck I'm not either," I thought to myself. I knew better than to say that shit out loud. Jordan knocked on the door just in time.

"Hi Jordan," Aunt Trudy said as he kissed me hello.

"Hello Trudy, Sissy, Miss Gladys."

"Hi Jordan," Grandma said. "Sissy don't be rude – say hello."

"That's ok Miss Gladys – you ready Trenice?"

"Yes," I said as I stood up and headed for the door.

"We'll see ya later," Jordan said.

"By Grandma, Aunt Trudy, Sissy." I was so glad to get the fuck outta there. When we got in the cab I said, "I'm tellin' Grandma about the suit and here comes Aunt Trudy with that nosy bitch talking about we gettin' paid!"

"What?"

"Yea – she talkin' 'bout she know I'm gonna share with family – yea right – in her fuckin' dreams!" We both laughed as we headed to Jordan's house.

When we got to Jordan's house, Miss April and Miss June started right in.

"Hi Trenice – how's your foot?"

"This cast comes off in two weeks."

"They sure don't make beds like they used to huh?" Miss April said.

"They sure don't," Miss June said as they both bust out laughing. Jordan and I just shook our heads.

"Jordan I wanna stop and see my mother ok?"

"You want me to go with you?"

"Sure," I said. We went out in the hall and all you heard was 'thump, thump, thump' as my rubber heel hit the steps.

"Mommy – Trenice is here!" my little sister yelled as she opened the door. Jordan came in behind me.

"Are you the man that broke my sister's foot? Why did you do that?" My mother, brothers, and sisters all bust out laughing.

"It's not funny – he hurt my sister!" she cried.

"It's ok Shaliyah," I said as I hugged her.

"I'm sorry Shaliyah," Jordan said. "I didn't mean to hurt Trenice. I love her and I'll never hurt her again. Do you forgive me?"

"That's the same shit my Daddy said to me every time he hit my Mommy!" she screamed and ran into the room crying. Everyone got quiet. Jordan looked at me then at my mother. I got up to go in the room.

"Leave her alone Trenice," my mother said.

"No – I'm gonna talk to my sister."

"Trenice – you're mother's right," Jordan tried to explain but I cut him off...

"No she isn't right! Don't you see what just happened? We're all old enough to deal with this but she doesn't understand – all she knows is you're gonna do to me what my father did to my mother!" I had never yelled at Jordan like that before. We didn't see Shaliyah standing there...

"Stop it! Leave my Mommy alone!" she screamed."

"I'm sorry Shaliyah – I'm sorry," I cried as I hugged her.

"Don't cry Trenice, don't cry," she said.

"Maybe we better go Trenice," Jordan said.

"Maybe you're right," I said as I got we got up to leave.

"Sit down Trenice," my mother said. We sat down.

"You don't have to go anywhere. I wish I didn't put you all through that shit," she said with tears in her eyes.

"Mom it wasn't your fault...let's talk about something else."

"Ok," she said as she wiped her eyes. I told her all about the law suit as she made us coffee. My brothers and sisters just sat and listened.

"Good – I could use a new car," she said. Jordan and I looked at each other and shook our heads. I got up from the table.

"Where you goin' Trenice?" my mother asked.

"I'm going to talk to Shaliyah Mom."

"Trenice don't upset her any more. She's been through enough."

"I know Mom but you need to get her some help."

"Don't tell me how to raise my child Trenice."

"I'm not Mom, but there's a play group in White Plains called the Stepping Stone. The children play and as they act out their aggressions, the social workers help them deal with their issues."

"What the hell do you know about a group like that?"

"They helped me a lot," I said as I went into the room to talk to Shaliyah.

"Hi Shaliyah. Can we talk?"

"Uh huh."

"Jordan didn't mean to hurt me Shaliyah. It was an accident."

"But Daddy always said that to Mommy Trenice."

"But Daddy hit Mommy – Jordan didn't hit me Shaliyah."

"He didn't?" she perked.

"No Shaliyah. We sat on the bed to go to sleep and the bed broke." I sat on her bed to show her what happened and I placed my foot between the bed and dresser to show her how it happened. "See Shaliyah?"

"Yea....Trenice?"

"Yes?"

"If you wanted to go to sleep, why didn't you just go back to Grandma's house? Then you wouldn't have broken your foot." I laughed to myself as she ran into the kitchen.

"Jordan lets go downstairs now ok?"

"Ok Trenice – By Miss Claire – nice to meet you all," he said.

"Bye Jordan," Shaliyah said as she gave him a hug.

"Bye Shaliyah," he said as he hugged her back and smiled. We left to go downstairs.

When we got out in the hallway Jordan said, "You wanna talk about what just happened?"

"No," I said. He pulled me close to him and held me for a few minutes.

"I'm sorry I yelled at you like that."

"It's ok – don't worry about it – what did you say to Shaliyah to make her so happy?"

"I told her the truth."

"You did? You told her everything?"

"She's only 9 Jordan."

"Oh – right. But what did you tell her?"

"I told her we sat on the bed to go to sleep and the bed broke."

"What did she say?"

"She said I should'a went home – then I wouldn't have broken my foot."

"Oh I see." We bust out laughing as I 'thumped' downstairs while Jordan followed.

When we got inside Miss April's house, Jordan pulled me close to him and began kissing my neck.

"Ahem!" Miss April and Miss June interrupted.

"Excuse us," we said in unison. We all laughed as Jordan walked me downstairs and put me in the cab.

Chapter 24

"Jordan go see that lawyer yet?"

"He's goin' today Grandma."

"Good – the sooner the better – and don't pay your Aunt Trudy no mind – you know she always lookin' to get something for nothin'."

"I know Grandma." Little did she know I had already taken that advice about a few people..."Grandma?"

"Yea Trenice?"

"What do you want me to buy you when I get paid?"

"Trenice you don't owe me anything."

"I know Grandma but can I buy you something? You've always been there for me and so many other people – you deserve something nice."

"Thank you baby but I don't want anything," she said as she kissed my forehead. Grandma should've known I wasn't payin' her any mind.

"Who is it?" she called out as she went to answer the door.

"Jordan." I hobbled to the door.

"You keep hobbling like that Trenice you gonna break that other foot," she said as she let Jordan in.

"Hi Miss Gladys," he said as he sat down.

"How'd everything go?" Grandma asked.

"It went ok. He said we should hear from them by next week. You ready Trenice?"

"Yup."

"Bye Miss Gadys."

"Bye Grandma."

"See ya later," Grandma called out from the bedroom.

After we got in the cab Jordan said, "Since I didn't have to work today, why don't we stop by Jake and Rachel's?"

"Ok." When we got there they were waiting outside. "They knew we were comin' didn't they?"

"Yea – I called them earlier. You mind?"

"No – we gonna stay here?"

"Nope."

"Where we goin'?"

"You'll see." A limo pulled up and Jake and Rachel got in the car. "C'mon Trenice," he said as he opened the door for me. I got in the car with them and we drove off. So far everything looked the same until we got to New York City. I noticed we were on the west side and we turned at 59th Street.

"Why are we going this way honey?"

"You'll see." We kept going until we stopped in front of the Mark Helinger Theatre.

"Surprise!" they all yelled.

"Thanks but what's the occasion?" Jordan pulled two tickets out of his jacket and handed them to me.

"Oh my God – Smokey Robinson?"

"Yes – Smokey Robinson." He helped me out the car and we went inside.

I fell asleep on the way home from the concert. When I woke up we were almost home. "Smokey Robinson gets better and better – I wish tonight didn't have to end," I said as we pulled up in front of Grandma's house."

"Maybe it doesn't have to end," Jordan whispered in my ear. We had dropped off Jake and Rachel so it was just the two of us.

"You two gettin' out here or can I take you somewhere?" For a minute I'd forgotten the limo driver was in the limo with us.

"I'll get out here," I said before Jordan could answer. He helped me out the limo and, as luck would have it, my Aunt Trudy's nosy bitch as friend, Sissy was right on time...

"Where you goin' all dressed up?"

"To bed," I said. I kept going until I got upstairs without looking back.

Chapter 25

It was Friday and I hadn't seen Jordan since Tuesday night. I missed him so much and I was tired of staying in the house.

"One more week and this stupid cast comes off – then I can get my life back," I thought to myself.

The phone rang and I snatched it up hoping it was Jordan. "Hello," I said cheerfully.

"Trenice its Tyler. I have some bad news."

"What's wrong?"

"Well, I don't know how to put this…but they laughed at your suit."

"They laughed?"

"I'm sorry Trenice. They offered to pay your medical bills and give you $20,000. That's it."

"Tyler?"

"Yes Trenice?"

"Can you set up a meeting with their lawyers?"

"Trenice they've made up their mind."

"I hear ya, but I've got an idea."

"What's that?"

"Well, I may not get $1,000,000 but they might be willing to settle if I threatened to go to the press."

"Trenice, that won't get you any money."

"I know it won't but by the time I get through telling my story to ABC, NBC, CBS, and CNN, how many people are gonna be willing to get a room for a night of romance at the Holiday Inn Crowne Plaza if they're afraid the bed will break? I don't think the Holiday Inn Crowne Plaza will like that kind of publicity."

"I like your idea Trenice. You may not get any money but this will ruin their reputation. Who knows – you could even get a book outta this," he laughed.

"I'll call you later this afternoon."

"Thanks Tyler."

"You're welcome Trenice."

"Hello," I said as I picked up the phone again.

"You don't sound too happy to hear from me."

"Jordan!"

"Now that's more like it! Now what's wrong?"

"Tyler just called."

"Well?"

"They offered to pay my medical bills and give me $20,000."

"Take it Trenice – it's better than nothing."

"I asked Tyler to set up a meeting with their lawyers. He's gonna call me back."

"Trenice you sure you wanna go ahead with this? Maybe you should take the money and run."

"Tyler thinks it's a good idea. He says I may not get any money but it could ruin their reputation."

"Why do it if you don't think you can get any money?"

"Jordan I know we won't get a million dollars but we could get more than $20,000."

"We could also get nothing."

"If I settle for $20,000, after the law firm takes 33% plus their fees, it will be as if I settled for nothing."

"See what Tyler says when he calls you back – then we'll see."

"Ok Jordan."

"I gotta run..."

"Jordan?"

"Yes?"

"I love you."

"I love you too Trenice."

"See you tonight?"

"See you tonight."

I sat there staring at the phone all misty eyed.

"Whatsa matter with you?" Grandma asked as she came down the hall.

"Oh nothing," I sighed.

"I'll be glad when you get that damn cast off – you need to get outside and get some air..."

"Hello?" I snatched the phone up on the first ring.

"Trenice?"

"Yes Tyler?"

"They'll meet with us tomorrow morning."

"Wow that was quick."

"Don't get your hopes up Trenice. I like your idea but as your lawyer I must advise you that this may not work."

"I know Tyler. I appreciate everything you've done for me and your willingness to even take the case no matter what happens.

"Well I'm glad you appreciate me Trenice, but appreciation don't pay the rent," he laughed.

"I hear ya. What time tomorrow?"

"10 a.m."

"Ok – see ya then."

"Who you on the phone with now?" Grandma asked as I called Jordan.

"I'm callin' Jordan Grandma."

"You need to let the man work Trenice."

"I know Grandma but this is important..."

"Aren't you gonna see him tonight?"

"Yea but..." I was totally unaware that Jordan had answered and heard this exchange...

"Helllooooo?"

"Oh sorry Jordan – Tyler called. We have an appointment tomorrow at 10 a.m."

"On Saturday?"

"That's what I said too."

"Ok – I'll see ya later then."

"Ok." After I hung up the phone I told Grandma about the meeting.

"You should've taken the $20,000 Trenice. Now you probably won't get anything," she said as she went down the hall.

Jordan came to pick me up after work.

"I'm glad you're here Jordan – if it weren't for you Trenice wouldn't go outside at all!"

"I know Miss Gladys. We'll see ya later."

I started to tell Grandma I didn't go outside 'cause I didn't feel like sitting outside with Aunt Trudy and nosy ass Sissy but I just kept quiet and left with Jordan.

When we got to Jordan's house I asked, "Jordan, can we go see my mother?"

"You sure?"

"Yea."

"Oooookkkaaayyy...," he said as I 'thumped' upstairs. When we got to the top of the stairs Jordan pulled me close to him and began nibbling on my neck.

"Oooohhhh... Mommy, Trenice and Jordan are kissing!" Shaliyah yelled as she came up the stairs. We jumped when we heard her.

"Shaliyah!" I breathed, "You scared me!"

"Tee hee hee...," she said as she knocked on the door.

"Hello Jordan, Hello Trenice, come on in," my mother said.

"Hello Miss Claire."

"Mommy I saw Jordan and Trenice kissing," Shaliyah said.

"Uh huh, that's how you wound up with that cast on your foot," my mother laughed.

"No it isn't Mommy," Shaliyah said. We all turned around to look at her. I was praying my mother wouldn't correct her and go into a lengthy explanation – sometimes parents give their children too much information too soon, or too little information too late. I remember when my brothers were 9 and 10 and she'd tell them, "When you get older, don't listen to what the girl says – use a condom." When they'd ask, "Why?" she'd say, "You'll find out when you get older." What was the point in mentioning it if she wasn't going to explain it? Anyway, thank God she didn't try to correct Shaliyah.

"Mommy – I had so much fun today – and guess what Mommy? My friend Suzie goes there too!"

"That's good honey."

"Mom, where'd she go?" I asked as Shaliyah went to change her clothes.

"The Stepping Stone," she said. Jordan and I looked at each other and smiled.

"So what brings you here?" my mother asked.

"I spoke to Tyler today."

"What'd he say?" "

"Well Mom, they only offered to pay my medical bills and give me $20,000. We have a meeting tomorrow morning with their lawyers at 10 a.m."

"Trenice maybe you should've accepted their offer."

"We'll see what happens tomorrow Mom."

"Don't get your hopes up Trenice."

"I won't Mom don't worry. Besides, how can I buy you a car with $5,000?"

"$5,000? What happened to $20,000?"

"33% plus fees goes to my lawyer," I said.

"You mean 65%," my mother said as we all laughed.

"Mom, it's gettin' late and I wanna go see Miss April and Miss June before I go."

"Alright – tell them I said hello."

"I will Mom – good night."

"Good night."

"Good night Miss Claire," Jordan said.

"Bye Trenice, bye Jordan!" Shaliyah yelled.

"Bye Shaliyah!" we yelled back.

Miss April heard me 'thumpin' downstairs and opened the door. "You can't sneak up on nobody can ya?" she laughed.

"Hi Miss April" I said as we went into the house.

"Hi Mum-Mum," Jordan said. I laughed when Miss April told me how when Jordan was little they tried to teach him to say Grandma and Mamma but all he could say was Mum-Mum - and he's been calling them both Mum-Mum ever since.

We told Miss April and Miss June about my conversations with Tyler.

"I'm glad you didn't accept the $20,000 – you'll probably get more," Miss April said. I couldn't believe my ears.

"Huh? You're the first person to tell me that Miss April – even Jordan said I should've taken the $20,000."

"Trenice was smart not to take that money," Miss June said.

"Why Mum?"

"Because you never take the first offer. I worked for the County Attorney's office for 20 years. If they offer you $20,000 they can go as high as $50,000."

"Wow!" I screamed.

"Calm down Trenice – I don't want you to get your hopes up. I'm just sayin' that if they offered you twenty, thay can go a little higher." Visions of dollar signs danced in my head...

"Trenice, I better get you home – we have an interesting day tomorrow."

"Ok – good night Miss April, good night Miss June."

"See ya in a bit Mum-Mum."

When we got to Grandma's house, Aunt Trudy and nosy ass Sissy were sitting outside.

"You hear from that lawyer yet?" Sissy yelled to the whole building.

"Not yet," I lied. Jordan and I hurried into the building and up the stairs so we wouldn't have to carry on a conversation. Soon as we got in the house here comes Aunt Trudy right behind us.

"Hey Jordan."

"Hey Trudy."

"Trenice you ain't hear from that lawyer yet?"

"No," I lied.

"Trenice I thought you said you had an appointment tomorrow at 10 a.m.," Grandma yelled.

Shit! – I was almost caught – then I had an idea: "No Grandma – I called and they said he was in court and he wouldn't be available until after 10 a.m. tomorrow."

"Oohh."

"Ma, come outside – me and Sissy sittin' downstairs," Aunt Trudy said.

"Ok – soon as I get out the bathroom," Grandma said.

When Grandma went outside I said, "Jordan you better go before my Grandma comes back with Aunt Trudy, Sissy, and more questions," I laughed.

"You're right – good night."

"Good night – I love you."

"I love you too." I got in bed and pretended to be asleep when Grandma, Sissy, and Aunt Trudy came in the house, gossiping about the commotion outside.

Chapter 27

Jordan came to pick me up for an early breakfast Saturday morning. It was perfect – I got out of the house while everyone was still asleep. Even the neighbors sleep late on Saturday, so we were good to go...or so I thought...

"What chall doin' up so early?"

"Hi Sissy," I said. "Shit – where the fuck did she come from?" I thought to myself...then I saw the laundry cart..."I see you doin' laundry."

"Yea girl – gotta git them machines before 12:00 – where y'all off too?"

"Breakfast."

"Alright – see ya later."

"Ok Sissy," I said as we got in the cab.

"Whew – that was a close one huh?"

"50 Main Street, White Plains," Jordan told the driver. "Let's just do this – then we can eat."

"Sounds good to me," I said.

We got to Tyler's office at 10 a.m. sharp. "C'mon Trenice – let's hurry up," Jordan said.

"They can wait a minute," I said.

"Good morning Trenice, Jordan – this is Bernice Thomas and Gordan Smith," Tyler said as he introduced us. "They represent the Holiday Inn Crowne Plaza."

"Good morning, good morning," we said as we all shook hands and sat down. Tyler's secretary came into the room.

"Coffee anyone?"

"Yes please," I said. She brought in a coffee pot, cups, creamer, sugar, and spoons then she cracked the door. I could see her listening but I didn't mind. I just hoped she didn't get caught. The court reporter prepared her machine and we began.

After the 'state your name and address for the record, etc.' Bernice spoke. "Miss Robertson, Mr. Williams we've gone over your papers and I'm sorry but our offer stands. Take it or leave it." Now the fun was to begin.

"Your offer stands? I wish your mattress stood like your offer – then maybe we wouldn't be spending Saturday morning in this fuckin' office..."

Bernice's eyes damn nearly popped out of her head along with Tyler's and Jordan's.

"Miss Robertson, please," Gordon interjected.

"Please what? Huh?"

I got so close to that man Jordan and Tyler stood up at the same time. Jordan put his hand on my shoulder and Tyler sat back down. I remained standing, but I was nowhere through...

"Please what?!" I got even louder. "Please forget that I could've broken my back? Please forget that the hotel staff and paramedics saw me sprawled out ass out? Please forget that I got a permanent fuckin' scar on my forehead? Is that what you want me to do? Huh? You want me to pretend I don't have the fuckin' cast on my foot? Huh?"

Bernice and Gordon began to back away from me as I continued ranting and raving at the top of my lungs...

"You want me to forget about that fuckin' concussion I got? Huh? You want me to forget all the ridiculing I've had to put up with? Huh? All the fuckin' bed jokes? You want me to forget about my lost wages? Oh I got disability – fuckin' $250 for one month but I should be glad right? Well fuck that and fuck both of you 'cause that's about all I've been able to do for the past 5 weeks!"

Tyler and Jordan were stunned. I could hear Tyler's secretary laughing outside the door. No one said anything – they just sat there while the court reporter got it all down, so I started up again.

"Ya know, it would've been nice if you pretended to give a damn – maybe even offer a fake ass apology, but no – that would have been too humane!"

"Maybe this wasn't such a good idea," Bernice said.

"Oh it was a great idea," I said.

They all looked perplexed.

"I bet ABC, NBC, CBS, and CNN will think it's a great idea too. How many people do you think will wanna stay at the Holiday Inn Crowne Plaza after they get a hold of this story?"

"Perhaps we were a little insensitive Miss Robertson. We do, at the very least, owe you an apology," Bernice said.

"Yes – it appears you have suffered a great deal," Gordon said.

"It appears? What – you need fuckin' glasses?!" I was up on my feet so fast Tyler and Jordan got up and Jordan stepped in front of me... "Miss Thomas was right – this was a complete waist of time – let's go Jordan," I said as I got up to get my coat...

"Miss Robertson – wait...," Bernice said. "Perhaps we could make you another offer..."

I sat back down while Bernice and Gordon whispered to each other. Then Bernice leaned over and whispered something to Tyler. Tyler wrote something on a piece of paper and handed it to me. I looked at the paper and smiled. Jordan looked at me then at the paper. He smiled as he read the following amounts: $500,000, $100,000. He handed me back the paper and I handed it back to Tyler. I nodded in agreement but didn't smile. Jordan was looking at me as if to say, "What's wrong?"

"My clients have agreed to your offer," Tyler said as he winked at me.

"Very good. We'll have the papers in your office next week," Bernice said as she and Gordon stood up. They walked out without saying good bye. Jordan looked at me.

"Aren't you happy?"

"They gone yet?" I asked.

"Yes, they're gone," Tyler said.

"Woooo hooo!" I yelled and we all gave each other high fives. Tyler's secretary came flyin' into the office...

"You go girl!"

"You go boy!" I shouted as I gave Tyler a high 5. Jordan picked me up, spun me around, and gave me a big kiss.

"You did good Trenice. I swear you had me worried for a minute."

"Good – that was the whole idea. I knew if you were worried, they were worried."

"We got lucky Trenice – really lucky," Tyler said.

"Girl, when you said I wish your mattress stood like your offer I was on the floor crackin' up!" his secretary laughed.

"That was a good one Trenice," Tyler said as they all laughed.

"I got their fuckin' attention."

"Especially when Gordon said 'appears' and you asked him if he needed fuckin' glasses," Jordan laughed. "I thought you were about to go to jail for assault!"

"Shit – we all did," Tyler laughed.

"The papers should be here next Friday, latest. Have a great day – you earned it."

"We will – and thanks for everything Tyler."

Chapter 28

Once Jordan and I got into the limo I let out a big sigh of relief. "Whew! We did it!"

"You did it Trenice," Jordan said as he pulled me into another kiss.

We spent the whole day dinning and shopping, courtesy of MasterCard, Visa, American Express, and Discover.

"At least we won't have to worry about how we're gonna pay these bills next month," Jordan said as we both laughed. I had been oblivious to the pain in my ankle until we sat down for an early dinner. Jordan noticed me rubbing my lower leg.

"You alright Trenice?"

"I'll be ok – I guess I over did it a little."

"After we eat let's get you home. You don't need to re-injure your foot just when the cast is ready to come off."

"You're right."

We finished our meal, dessert, and Jordan wrapped his arm around me as I limped out to the limo. "Wait here – I'll be right back," he said after he put me in the limo. He flew down the street and was back in a few minutes.

"Where'd you go?" Jordan handed me a paper bag from the pharmacy. I looked inside and there was a bottle of ibuprofen – 400 milligrams each.

"Thank you, thank you, thank you," I said as I swallowed two of them on the spot. I stretched out in the back seat as Jordan picked up my feet and placed them in his lap. He rubbed my legs until I fell asleep.

We stopped at Char's house first and gave her the news. "You go girl!" she said as we high-fived each other laughing. "I can't believe it – I would'a took the $20,000 and ran" Char said.

"I almost did – but then I thought about everything I went through and Jordan's grandmother told me not to accept their first offer."

"She did?"

"Yep. She said you never take the first offer – if they offer you twenty, they can go as high as fifty."

"No shit – you got $50,000?!"

"No they didn't go that high."

"How much did you get?"

Jordan and I looked at each other.

"Well?" Char asked.

"We got $600,000," I said.

"Oh my God! What are you gonna do with all that money?"

"I'm gonna put it in a trust fund so I can't fuck it up," I said real quick. "Well, I've had a long day Char, so I'm gonna go."

"Alright girl – your cast comes off next week right?"

"Right," Jordan answered with a mischievous grin.

When we got to Jordan's house I said, "Can we go see my mother first?"

"You sure you up to it?"

"Yea."

"Ok – let's go." I started 'thumping' upstairs and Miss April opened the door...

"That you Trenice?"

"Yea Mum – we goin' upstairs – we'll be down in a few," Jordan said.

"Ok," she said as she closed her door. When we got upstairs my brothers and sisters were waiting.

"We heard you 'thumpin' up them steps," they laughed as they opened the door.

"Mom, Trenice and Jordan are here," Marlowe said as we sat in the kitchen.

"Hi Trenice, Hi Jordan – how'd it go today?"

"I took the settlement Mom."

"You did?" she asked. As she looked at me Jordan gave me a look too, but no one noticed. Then he caught on...

"Yea, she figured she better take it while it was on the table before they changed their mind."

"Good idea Trenice – no sense in being greedy – be grateful for what you can get."

"Ma, I've had a long day and my ankle hurts so I'm gonna go ok?"

"Ok – take care."

"Bye everybody," I said as I left.

"Bye Trenice, Jordan," they said. I 'thumped" downstairs to Jordan's house.

"You didn't ask for more money?" Miss June asked as we told her we settled.

"No Miss June – she was a real bitch – oh excuse my language Miss April, Miss June."

"That's ok honey," Miss April said.

"Well I still think you should'a asked for more, but it's over with now."

Before Jordan could say anything I said, "Well, I better go get off this foot."

"We'll see you later Mum-Mum."

"Ok – get home safe," Miss April said.

"Congratulations," Miss June said."

"Thanks – good night."

"You don't want anybody to know how much money we really got, do you?" Jordan asked as we got in the limo.

"They'll find out soon enough – besides we haven't even got the check yet – we don't need anyone telling us how to spend it."

"True."

Soon as we got to Grandma's house we got upstairs without seeing anyone. We thought we were in the clear until we got in the house.

"Trenice, your lawyer called. He said to tell you the checks would be ready Friday afternoon. How much did you get?" Grandma asked. Damn! Bad enough Aunt Trudy wouldn't let me get a word in, but her nosy ass friend, Sissy was sitting right there all smiles waiting for an answer, along with my grandmother.

"I won't know until he takes his fees out. I'll probably end up with a couple thousand."

"Damn that's it?" Aunt Trudy asked.

"Yea well, lawyers are expensive, and besides – I gotta pay for all these clothes," I said pointing at the bags.

"Well something's better than nothing, but I hope you didn't spend it all before you got it."

"Me too Aunt Trudy."

"Alright Ma – we'll see you later."

"Ok Trudy."

When they left she said, "How much money are you gettin' Trenice? Really?"

"I really won't know until next week Grandma." I didn't lie to her but I wasn't about to tell her either.

"I'll see ya soon Trenice – you look tired," Jordan said.

"I am Jordan," I said as I kissed him good night.

"I love you."

"I love you too."

Chapter 29

Jordan and I had been talking back and forth on the phone since last Sunday but I hadn't seen him. I missed him so much it hurt. I couldn't believe I was finally on my way to get this cast off. When I got to White Plains Hospital, I didn't have to wait long.

"C'mon in Trenice, Dr. Campton said as I 'thumped' into the office. He laughed as he helped me up on the table. "So far it looks good," he said as he cut the cast off. He picked up my foot and examined it as I wiggled my toes. "Trenice, I'm going to send you for another x-ray just to make sure your foot's healed properly. If all looks good, you can go home, but don't wear any heels for another two weeks. There might be a little tenderness but a few ibuprofens should take care of that.

"Thank you Dr. Campton."

"Trenice?"

"Yes Dr. Campton?"

"Stay away from the Holiday Inn," he laughed as he closed the door. I waited for a few and the technician escorted me to the radiology department. He looked down and saw I had on my sneakers.

"Oh – you walkin' on your foot already?"

"Yea – it's ok."

"Well you're probably fine, but let's get a look at your x-ray to make sure."

"Ok." After I had the x-ray the technician looked it over.

"You're fine Trenice – I'll send this up to Dr. Campton. Have a good day."

"Thanks," I said as I made a beeline outta there.

When I got to Yonkers I went straight to Jordan's job. "You got the cast off – it looks good! You sure you're ok?"

"Yes – I'm fine – I feel like my old self."

"What did the doctor say?"

"He said no heels for another two weeks, take ibuprofen for pain, and stay away from the Holiday Inn." All his co-workers laughed.

"Alright Bob – we out," Jordan said as we went towards the exit.

"I guess I gotta deal with that when I go back to work," I said as we got in the cab.

"I guess you do," Jordan said as he got in beside me.

When we got to Tyler's office, everyone was all smiles. "C'mon in Jordan, Trenice," Tyler said as he escorted us into his office. When we sat down he popped a bottle of champagne, poured 3 small cups, and we toasted to our success.

"Here's to us," we all said. Tyler handed Jordan and I a check for $50,000 each. After he took $150,000, we had Tyler purchase 4 tickets for an all-expense-paid two-week cruise to Bermuda for Miss April, Miss June, my mother, and my grandmother. They would all go on the cruise at the same time – the ship was leaving from New York City the 2nd week of October. We also had Tyler purchase 3 tickets for an all-expense-paid 7 day/6 night cruise to the Bahamas for Char, Jake, and Rachel, including tickets for Amtrak to Florida so they would be able to connect directly to their cruise ship. Jordan and I got round-trip airfare and hotel accommodations for 2 weeks in Hawaii for next year. The rest of the money was put into a joint checking account.

"Thanks again for everything Tyler. We couldn't have done it without you."

"My pleasure Trenice, my pleasure." Jordan and I both looked at each other. Tonight was the night. "And if you ever need me again, my door's always open." "Thanks again Tyler," I said as we left his office. I had no idea we would need his services again so soon.

Chapter 30

"Why don't we go to Jake and Rachel's house? We haven't seen them in a while," I said.

"Good idea," Jordan said as we walked to their house. When we got to their house, Rachel noticed right away...

"Your foot! The cast is gone! When did you get it off?"

"Earlier today."

"So what's been goin' on with the law suit?" Jordan and I looked at each other. He pulled the tickets out of his jacket and handed them to Jake.

"Oh wow honey – we're goin' to the Bahamas!"

"Oh my God – le'me see!"

"Oh my God – Oh my God," she screamed as they jumped up and down hugging.

They pulled us into the hug and I yelled, "Watch the foot!" as we all bust out laughing.

"So when did this get settled," Rachel asked.

"Last week – you should'a been there – I almost went to jail!"

"Oh my God what happened?" I let Jordan tell them. We were all laughing so hard we were holding our stomachs.

"Girl you are crazy," Jake said.

"Yea I had to get up a few times – I thought Trenice was gonna put her cast in that man's ass!" Jordan said. We hollered some more.

"Well, we gotta get goin," I said. "Where y'all goin'?" Jake teased.

"I know it's not the Holiday Inn," Rachel said. We all laughed.

When we got to Char's house and gave her the tickets she grabbed us both jumping up and down screaming, "Thank you – thank you –thank you!"

"You're welcome," Jordan laughed.

"Does your Grandma know yet?"

"No - we goin' to tell her now," I said.

"Alright I gotta work tonight so I'll talk to y'all later. Thank you – I love you," she yelled as we went downstairs.

"I love you too Char," I yelled back.

When we got to Grandma's house she had been waiting on us along with Aunt Trudy and Sissy. "Where you been all day Trenice? Oh my God – your cast is gone! You been takin' it easy on that foot right?"

"Yes Grandma."

"Hi Miss Gladys, Trudy, Sissy."

"Hi Jordan," they said.

"Grandma come upstairs – we got something for you." I might as well have invited Aunt Trudy and Sissy upstairs too 'cause they came right along with us. When we got in the house I gave my Grandma the envelope. She looked at the tickets and started to cry.

"Watcha go and do this for?" she said as she gave me a hug.

"Because I love you Grandma and you deserve it."

"Does your mother know yet?"

"No I'm going to give her her ticket when we leave here.

"What's the ticket for?" Aunt Trudy asked.

"Me and Claire are going to Bermuda for 2 weeks Trudy!" she beamed.

"Oh that's nice," Aunt Trudy said. I could tell she was disappointed.

"Yes that is nice Miss Gladys," Sissy said. "So what you do with the rest of your money?"

"I put it away. Grandma, we gotta go so we see ya later ok?"

"Ok Trenice." We left Aunt Trudy and Sissy sitting in the kitchen with Grandma.

When we got to my mother's house, Shaliyah answered the door. "Mommy Trenice doesn't have the cast on anymore!"

"Come on in Trenice, Jordan."

"Mom sit down. I have something for you." She sat down and we handed her the envelope as my brothers and sisters watched her open it. Her eyes got wide and she jumped up. "Hott damn – I'm going to Bermuda!"

"Mommy where's Bermuda?" Shaliyah asked.

"Mommy's going on vacation honey."

"Ohhh – can I go? Please?"

"No Shaliyah – not this time."

"But I wanna go, I wanna go," she cried.

"Shaliyah?"

"Yes Trenice?"

"How 'bout next week you go to Great Adventure?"

"Really?" she perked.

"Yes."

"Oh yea!" she said as she hugged me.

"Trenice don't have her waitin' if you not gonna take her."

"Oh I figured you were gonna take her Mom."

"Oh I guess you figured you were buyin' us tickets then?"

"Sure Mom." Since I volunteered it I guess it was the least I could do. "Mom we gotta go downstairs and see Miss April and Miss June ok?"

"Ok – I'll see y'all later."

"By Miss Claire," Jordan said.

"Bye Jordan."

When we got downstairs and knocked on the door Miss April was surprised. "No more cast I see – when you get it taken off?"

"I had it taken off this morning Miss April – Hi Miss June."

"Sit down Mum-Mum – we got something for ya." They both stared as Jordan handed them the envelope. When then realized what it was, they jumped up and down screaming, "We goin' to Bermuda – we goin' to Bermuda!"

Just then, there was a knock at the door. I'll get it," I said as I opened the door.

"Is Jordan here?"

"Who are you?" I asked.
"I'm Rosalind."

Chapter 31

"Who is it Trenice?" Jordan asked as he came to the door. When he saw it was Rosalind, his whole expression changed. "What do you want?!" he snapped.

"We need to talk Jordan. Alone."

I wasn't going to disrespect Miss April's house so I kept quiet but, "Bitch, who the fuck do you think you are," was right on the tip of my tongue.

"Rosalind we don't have anything else to talk about. This is Trenice," he said as he pulled me close to him.

"I'm sorry Jordan but we really do need to talk – just for a few minutes...please. That's all I ask." Before Jordan could answer, Miss April and Miss June came to the door. "Hi Miss April, hi Miss June."

"What are you doing here Rosalind?" Miss April asked.

"I need to speak to Jordan. It's important."

"Trenice, I'll be right back ok?"

"No it's not fuckin' ok!" I thought. But what else could he do? "Sure honey."

"You'll be here when I get back?"

"Of course!" No way was I leaving until I heard what that bitch had to say to my man...

"Ok then," he said as I watched him leave with Rosalind.

Just then I got a really uneasy feeling in the pit of my stomach and ran for the bathroom..."Ugh!!"

"Trenice, you alright?!" Miss April called to me in the bathroom. I broke out in a cold sweat. I couldn't go back at there just yet.

"I'm ok Miss April. Must'a been something I ate." When I came out the bathroom, Jordan was just coming in the door.

"What did she want Jordan?!" Miss April snapped. I guess Miss April liked her about as much as I did.

"Mum-Mum I can't talk about this right now. Trenice, can you stay with me a while?"

"Of course." Jordan pulled me close to him, put his head on my shoulder, and Miss April and Miss June stood there in shock as Jordan cried. I held him and let him cry without saying a word. Anger was building up inside me as I thought, "What the fuck did this bitch do to him?" I was scared and angry at the same time. When he stopped crying, Miss April and Miss June came over to him and hugged him. Neither of us said a word.

"Mum-Mum we'll be back later ok?"

"Ok," Miss April said. Jordan took my hand and we went downstairs. We walked until we got to the park.

Chapter 32

Jake and Rachel were waiting for us when we got to the park. "What's up Jordan? What'd she say?" they asked. We all sat own on the bench...

"Fuckin' bitch! I don't fuckin' believe this shit!" he yelled as he punched the bench so hard he scared me.

"What Jordan – what?" Jake asked.

"Now she wanna tell me she made a fuckin' mistake! She and Steven broke up. She found out that Steven's not her baby's daddy – I am – And get this – she wants us to get back together – she claims she still loves me – can you believe that shit?!"

"Oh my God!" Rachel screamed.

"Yo man – that's some fucked up shit," Jake said.

"What if it's true? I wanna be a part of my son's life but I don't want anything to do with her – she has the nerve to tell me she still loves me after she ended our marriage to be with that punk ass motherfucker – I hate that bitch!" he yelled as he pounded his fist into the bench.

"It's gonna be alright man," Jake tried to console him but Jordan jumped up,

"How the fuck is it gonna be alright?!!...I'm sorry Jake I don't mean to take it out on you," he said as he slumped back down on the bench and put his head in his hands...

"Its ok man – don't worry about it...."

"I don't think it's yours," I said. They all looked at me in disbelief.

"What makes you say that Trenice?" Jordan asked.

"Think about it. The first time she got pregnant, she told you she wasn't ready for a baby. Then she got an abortion without discussing it with you. If she thought there was a chance this baby was yours, she never would have asked you for a divorce to go be with Steven. Now she's telling you she loves you and she wants to get back together. If you went back to her and re-married her, even if the child isn't your biological child, she would be guaranteed alimony and child support." Everyone was quiet for a minute...

"Fuckin' bitch!" Jordan yelled as he pounded his fist into the bench again.

"Jordan, she may be right," Jake said.

"But how can I prove it? Jordan asked. "I won't know until the baby's born!"

"You tell her you don't think it's your baby. She will take you to court. You won't have to pay for the paternity test because you're denying the child." I said.

"But what if it is mine Trenice? What are we gonna do?"

"We'll get through it together Jordan."

Jordan grabbed me by the face and said, "I love you," as he pulled me into a kiss.

"I love you too."

Chapter
33

I called Char when I got home.

"I can't believe she tryin' to pull some shit like that," Char said. "I bet you right – it probably ain't even his."

"But what if it is his Char?"

"You gonna stay with him?"

"Like white on rice!" I laughed. "So how's your love life Char?"

"Girl, it's better than ever. His divorce is final in two weeks. I'm takin' him on that cruise you gave me."

"I'm glad you're so happy Char."

"Me too girl – me too."

"Well, I gotta go girl, I've had a long, long day."

"Alright girl, keep me posted."

"I will Char."

Grandma came down the hall and saw me sitting at the table crying. "What's wrong Trenice?" I told her all about Rosalind and what I thought. "Oh my poor baby," Grandma said as she hugged me and I cried some more. "Don't you worry – it'll all work out. You love him right?"

"Hell yea! – Oh sorry Grandma."

"He loves you?"

"Yea!"

"Then that's all you need..."

The phone startled us both..."Hello?"

"Trenice, I just got off the phone with Rosalind. She's hot right about now."

"Too fuckin' bad – oh sorry Gramdna – you two would still be married if it weren't for the shit she did to you."

"Yea, she's takin' me to court just like you said she would."

"Good – then this will get settled the right way."

"Yes it will. I told Mum-Mum what happened. My grandmother told your mother. I hope that's alright."

"Sure it is – I was gonna tell her anyway."

"I'll talk to you soon Trenice. I love you."

"I love you too."

Chapter 34

I went back to work on Monday. Everyone was glad to see me. They had a 'Welcome Back' banner and a cake with a bed and some little person lying in the bed with a cast on. The bed was cracked in half. "I'm never gonna live this down," I said to myself.

Jordan came to pick me up from work like he used to. He showed me court papers he had received in the mail.

"Bitch doesn't waste any time does she?" I asked.

"I guess not."

"Jordan she had these papers filed before she talked to you. She came to see you on Saturday and you get papers today. She probably filed them last week."

"She probably did Trenice."

We went to get dinner and walked to Carvel for dessert. It was nice to be able to walk again. We met Jake and Rachel at the park and Jordan told them about the papers.

"She filed them shits last week," Rachel said.

"We wanna be there when you go to court," Jake said.

"I want you to be there," Jordan said.

When I got home I told Grandma about the papers and what I thought.

"You're probably right Trenice." I didn't see Aunt Trudy standing there.

"Why you buttin' into this Trenice? You have nothing to do with it." Grandma and I spun around...

"Whatchu mean she has nothing to do with this?"

"She doesn't Ma – its's between Rosalind and Jordan – she should mind her own business."

I was so mad I was about to say something but Grandma handled it for me..."Trudy, Rosalind may be your friend but what Rosalind did was fucked up! I'm glad Trenice is telling Jordan what to do and standing by him."

"I gotta go Ma – bye!" she said as she slammed the door.

"I don't give a damn if she is mad Trenice – you did the right thing."

"Thank you Grandma. Hello?" I asked as I answered the phone.

"Trenice, this is Tyler returning your call. How's everything?"

"Not so good Tyler." I explained everything that was going on.

"You did the right thing by calling me Trenice. He shouldn't show up in court without an attorney. Has he thought about what he's going to do if the child turns out to be his?"

"He's going to do the right thing Tyler."

"I'll see ya tomorrow Trenice."

"See ya tomorrow."

Chapter 35

We went to see Tyler first thing Tuesday morning. "I'm glad Trenice called me Jordan. It wouldn't look good for you to show up without an attorney – especially if the child turns out to be yours. I went over all the papers. Have you had your blood test yet?"

"We're going as soon as we leave here," Jordan said.

"Good. Re-read your statement and make sure you didn't leave anything out."

Jordan read the statement over and handed it back to Tyler. "It looks good," he said as he handed him back the papers.

"Ok – I'll talk to you next week."

"Thanks again Tyler," I said.

"My pleasure," Tyler said.

Jordan and I looked at each other and left without saying a word.

When we got to the hospital we went to the lab for the blood test. As we were going in, Aunt Trudy and Rosalind were coming out of the lab. We all just looked at each other. "Hi Aunt Trudy," I said. She just walked right past me like she didn't hear me, along with Rosalind. Oh well. I sat and waited while they took Jordan's blood.

"The court will get these results in 48 hours," the nurse said. Perfect. We were due back in court on Friday.

We met Jake and Rachel in the park later that evening. "She walked right past Trenice like she didn't even see her," Jordan told Jake.

"Don't even worry about it Trenice," Rachel said.

"I don't really care about my Aunt Trudy – I just want us to get this over with so Jordan and I can get back to our lives."

"I want that too Trenice," Jordan said.

When I got home my mother was there and so was Aunt Trudy. "Hi Mom, hi Aunt Trudy."

"Hi Trenice," my mother said.

"Trudy you have no business treatin' Trenice like that," Grandma said.

"I gotta go," she said as she slammed the door.

"Don't worry about her Trenice – she'll get over it," my mother said.

"Mom, all I want is for this to be over so Jordan and I can get back to our own lives."

"What if the child is his Trenice?"

"Then we have a child Mom." She and Grandma smiled at each other.

"I gotta get goin' Ma. – I'll see ya soon. Don't forget those tickets Trenice – Shaliyah's been buggin' me ever since you brought it up."

"The tickets were mailed to you Ma – you should get them by this weekend."

"Oh ok – bye Ma," my mother said as she hugged Grandma.

"Bye Claire."

"Hang in there Trenice," she said as she hugged me. It had been a long time since my mother hugged me and I needed it.

"I love you Ma."

"I love you too Trenice... I'm so proud of you." Tears came to my eyes. My mother hasn't said that to me since I was a child.

"Cut it out Trenice," she said as she hugged me again. We both laughed.

When my mother left I called Char to give her the latest. "How the fuck is your aunt gonna get mad and not speak to you 'cause his ex-wife is a hoe? Fuckin' stupid bitch!"

"I know – I don't understand it either – it's not like I'm telling Jordan anything wrong – she even gets mad when my Grandma tells her she ain't right."

"What's she gonna do when this is over? I know that's her friend, but you're her niece."

"Well she doesn't see it like that Char. But the only one I really care about is Jordan. This is tearing him up inside."

"When do you go back to court?"

"We go on Friday." I said. "Well le'me go – we gotta get up in the morning."

"Alright I'll talk to ya later," Char said. "Bye."

Chapter 36

It took forever for Friday to get here. I got up early and went to Jordan's house. "Hi Trenice, come on in," Miss April said as she opened the door. It was a house full. Miss April, Miss June, Jake, Rachel, my mother, Jordan, and I were squeezing past each other. Jordan grabbed me and gave me a hug.

"I love you Trenice."

"I love you too Jordan. No matter what happens, you got me."

We started kissing and Miss April said, "Y'all don't have time for that – we gotta get goin'." We all went downstairs and my mother got in the cab with Jordan and I – Miss April and Miss June got in the car with Jake and Rachel. When we pulled up in front of the court house, Char was standing there waiting for us.

"Thanks for coming Char," Jordan said.

"You know I was comin'," she said she hugged us both.

"Nice to see you again Char," my mother said.

"Good morning Miss Claire," Char said.

"Char, this is Miss April and Miss June – Jordan's grandmother and Jordan's mother," I said as I introduced them.

"C'mon Mum-Mum," Jordan said to them as we all got in the elevator and went upstairs.

When we got upstairs Tyler was waiting for us. "Tyler this is Miss April, Miss June, my mother Claire, my best friend Char, and Jordan's best friends Jake and Rachel. Just then Grandma came out the ladies room...

"Grandma!" I shouted.

"You didn't think you was gonna be here without me did you?" she said as she hugged me.

"Tyler this is my grandmother Gladys."

"Pleased to meet you Gladys – lets go inside."

When we got inside we saw Rosalind. Her attorney was none other than that fuckin' bitch, Bernice Thomas – the same one that represented the Holiday Inn with Gordon Smith. We all stood there for a minute...

"Everyone, this is Bernice Thomas – she's one of the attorneys that represented the Holiday Inn at my hearing," I said. Everyone bust out laughing.

Tyler smiled and said, "Nice to see you again Bernice." She went inside with Rosalind without responding.

Aunt Trudy and her nosy ass friend, Sissy, came off the elevator. "What the fuck is Sissy doing here?" I thought to myself..."Char, this is my Aunt Trudy and her friend Sissy."

"Nice meeting you," Char said. Neither one of them spoke.

The court officer came out..."Rosalind Williams vs Jordan Williams," she announced. We all went into the court room. Bernice, Rosalind, Aunt Trudy, and Sissy sat on the left. We all sat on the right. After all the swearing-ins and the testimony I sat on the edge of my seat waiting to hear what we came for. Judge Reynolds removed the results from the envelope..."Mr. and Mrs. Williams, will you step forward?" I didn't like that shit. As far as I was concerned, I was Mrs. Williams. "Mr. Williams when it comes to the unborn child, baby Williams...**YOU ARE NOT THE FATHER.**" Everyone was quiet. I was happy and sad at the same time. This should have been a happy time for Jordan, but it was anything but...

"You fuckin' bitch! I never should've married you – you put me through all this shit for nothing!"

"Mr. Williams I'm warning you..." Judge Reynolds said.

"Who's the father Rosalind? Do you even know?"

"I'm sorry Jordan... I thought..."

"You tried to fuckin' set me up – I fuckin' hate you!"

"Mr. Williams – one more outburst like that from you and you'll be escorted outta here in handcuffs!" Judge Reynolds yelled.

Tyler put his hand on Jordan's shoulder. "It's over now Jordan. Let it go. It's not worth it."

"Listen to him honey," Miss April said. You don't need to be goin to jail behind this. Let's go home."

I pulled Jordan to me from behind. He turned around and put his head on my shoulder. "We wasted so much time – all for nothing."

"It's over now Jordan – let's just go," I said. Bernice, Aunt Trudy, Sissy, and Rosalind left first. We all left after them. When we got downstairs I said, "I'm hungry – let's go get breakfast."

"Sounds good – sounds good," they all said.

"Tyler you comin' right?" Jordan asked.

"Afraid not – I gotta be back in court later today."

"C'mon Tyler – at least have a cup of coffee," I said. Miss April gave him a 'don't even try and say no' look.

"Ok, but just coffee," he said. We had a good breakfast but Jordan was quiet. After we finished breakfast Jake and Rachel offered to take Miss April, Miss June, and my mother home, but they decided to walk because it was such a nice day. Tyler had his cup of coffee with us and left about ½ hour ago so it was Jake, Rachel, Jordan, my grandmother, and me. Char had to go to work and Jake and Rachel had already made plans so they offered to take Grandma home.

When they were leaving I asked Grandma, "Do you think Aunt Trudy will ever speak to me again?"

"Only time will tell Trenice," she said.

"Alright – see ya later – we gotta get goin'," Jake said.

I gave Grandma a hug and a kiss, helped her in the car, and went back in the diner with Jordan.

We sat at the booth and Jordan didn't say anything.

"You ok honey?"

"I guess. I just can't believe she put me through all that. I loved her so much. I just don't get it. And there was a chance that was my child. I actually was prepared for that. I didn't want to believe that she was sleeping with someone else too. I thought Steven was the only one. In a way, I wanted you to be wrong – in a way I wanted that child to be mine so I wouldn't see my marriage for what it really was – nothing. Does that make sense Trenice?"

I took his hand, placed it in mine, and said, "It makes perfect sense."

We decided to walk back to Grandma's house. When we got upstairs, we could hear Aunt Trudy and Sissy inside...

"I bet she real happy now," Aunt Trudy said.

"She and Jordan probably somewhere celebratin' talkin' 'bout how stupid we are," Sissy said.

"I just can't believe Rosalind went out like that. I just knew Jordan was the father. I actually feel sorry for her. You know what Sissy?"

"What Trudy?"

"When Jordan first started seeing Trenice, I didn't know he was divorced. I told Trenice he was married and I worked with his wife. Here I was tryin' to protect Trenice from him and the whole time, he needed to be protected from Rosalind." They laughed along with my Grandma. A funny feeling came over me. I had just heard my Aunt Trudy say she was tryin' to protect me. I opened the door and went inside...

"Thank you Aunt Trudy – I love you," I said as I gave her a hug."

"What was that for?" she asked. Even Sissy and Grandma Looked perplexed.

"For being you Aunt Trudy. For being you." Grandma smiled at me and nodded. She was right. Or so I thought...

"Hello Trudy, Sissy," Jordan said as I went down the hall to change.

"Hello Jordan," they said.

I smiled to myself. "This is gonna be a good day after all," I thought. When I came back out into the living room, I had a brown suitcase with a few things in it.

"Watcha got in the suitcase?" Sissy asked.

"A little bit o' this – a little bit o'that," I said.

"You got a nightie in there Trenice?" Grandma asked as we all laughed.

"See ya later Grandma, bye Aunt Trudy, by Sissy."

"Bye Miss Gladys, Trudy, Sissy," Jordan said.

"Trenice?"

"Yes Grandma?"

"Should I put the chain on the door tonight?"

Jordan and I looked at each other. Aunt Trudy and Sissy looked at me, waiting for my answer. "Yes Grandma." Jordan looked at me and smiled. We left without saying another word.

When we got downstairs I told Jordan, "When you get home, pack your bag – I'm kidnapping you for the weekend."

"Sounds like a plan," he said as we made a beeline to his house. When we got upstairs Miss April opened the door. "I was wondering if I was gonna see you tonight," she said as Jordan began to hurry around the house, packing an overnight bag.

"Where y'all goin'," Miss June asked.

"Well we know they' not goin' to the Holiday Inn," Miss April said as we all laughed. Jordan zipped up his bag and gave them both a kiss goodbye.

"See you Sunday Mum-Mum."

"Monday," I corrected. Miss April and Miss June looked at us then at each other.

"See you Monday," he said as we left.

"Bye Miss April, Bye Miss June," I said on the way downstairs. Soon as we got downstairs and outside we ran smack into my mother, Marlowe, and Shaliyah.

"Hi Trenice!" she yelled as she hugged me. "I had sooo much fun today! Where you goin' Trenice?" She was almost sad.

"I'm going on vacation Shaliyah." She began to pout. "Oh boy," I thought to myself. "This is the last thing I need." Thank God she didn't start crying.

"I'll miss you Trenice. You comin' back?"

"Yes, Shaliyah I'll be back."

"You promise?"

"Of course."

"Okay. Trenice?"

"Yes Shaliyah?"

"Thank you for the tickets."

"You're welcome Shaliyah."

"Good night Miss Claire, Marlowe, Shaliyah," Jordan said.

"Good night," they all said as they went into the building.

Jordan grabbed me and pulled me into a kiss. I looked back and tapped Jordan on the shoulder.

"Look up there," I said as I pointed. We laughed as we noticed that Miss April and Miss June and been looking out the window the whole time.

We got to the train station and caught the last Amtrak leaving the station. When I showed the conductor our tickets we were escorted to our sleeper.

"What time will we be arriving?" I asked.

"Let's see – you're going to Niagara Falls – about 8 a.m."

"Thank you," I said as Jordan took down the sleeper.

"Niagara Falls huh?" He didn't know where we were going and I couldn't keep it from him for 8 hours. The dining car was open so we went to get something to eat and sat at the table enjoying the scenery as we sped through the cities. I brought along my camcorder and while we were at the table we recorded bits of scenery, people walking back and forth, and on the way back to our sleeper, I recorded a man holding his baby girl. Both of them were sleeping so soundly I couldn't resist. His daughter was cradled in his arms and he was propped up against the window, stretched out in the seat. Jordan waited patiently while I recorded about a minute of this then he followed me back to our sleeper. That was our cue to get some sleep.

Chapter 38

When we got to Niagara Falls on Saturday morning, check in wasn't until 2 p.m. so we checked in our bags and went on an all day cruise which included breakfast and lunch. After a day of site seeing, we were ready to check into the hotel. I had been very specific when I made the reservations and when we got to the room, I was happy to see that they followed my request to the letter. The room was much like the room we had at the Holiday Inn Crown Plaza with a few exceptions:

Instead of a chandelier hanging from the ceiling, there was a ceiling fan. Plush navy blue carpeting soothed our aching feet and white furniture trimmed in powder blue complemented the powder blue walls and carpet. There was a table for two, also white trimmed in powder blue, with chairs to match.

Jordan smiled when he saw this. There was a little kitchenette with a dishwasher, refrigerator, and a Jacuzzi in the middle of the room. The walls were mirrored from top to bottom.

The bathroom was powder blue, with white towels trimmed in powder blue with plush navy blue carpeting and a Jacuzzi for 2, including a shower – just like at the Holiday Inn. Jordan turned on the hot water, went to open the suitcase, found the seashell and the powder blue bath salts, came back into the bathroom, and placed some of them in the Jacuzzi. After the Jacuzzi was full, Jordan turned off the water, we both got undressed, and we slid into the Jacuzzi and let the water soothe our backs for the next hour while splashing water all over each other and the tile floor.

"You hungry?" Jordan asked.

"Yes," I said as we laughed, climbed out the Jacuzzi, cleaned up the water, put on our robes, and ordered room service. We ordered steak, shrimp for me, chicken for him, baked potatoes, string beans, Caesar salad, Pepsi, bottle water for the fridge, and apple crisp with caramel and vanilla ice cream for dessert. We finished dinner and dessert, cleaned up, and fell asleep holding each other while the television watched us.

Chapter 39

"Hello Miss Gladys," Jordan said when we got back.

"Hi Jordan – where's Trenice?"

"She's coming in now," he said as he held the door open for me.

"Oh my God Trenice – how in the hell did you break your leg?" I hobbled in with the crutches as Grandma, my mother, Aunt Trudy, and Sissy looked at us in shock.

"Y'all break another bed Trenice?" Sissy sneered as everyone else laughed.

"What hotel you suin' this time?" They all hollered when my mother asked that question.

"We didn't break any beds and we're not suing anyone," I said as I sat down.

"What happened Trenice?" I had to make this good. Grandma could glare right through you and you had better not so much as flinch – let alone lie! Oh well – here goes....

"Jordan warned me to be careful but you know how stubborn I can be..." Jordan's eyes got wide as quarters and before I could say anything else he jumped in...

"Miss Gladys I can explain..."

"Shut up and let Trenice talk – her mouth works just fine...go ahead Trenice..." Jordan looked at me pleading for me not to tell them with his eyes...

"We went outside at 4:30 a.m. to see the sun come up..."

"Yea?"

"Well it was so pretty I wanted to get a better picture..."

"So?'"

"So I told Jordan to hold on to me so I could lean over the bar and get a better picture..."

"What bar Trenice?" Sissy asked - then she got all up in my face. I swear if it wasn't for my grandmother I'da told Sissy to get the fuck outta my face – bad enough Grandma was giving me the 3rd degree in front of this bitch – but she had to be up in my face too?

"Jordan, can you give me that hanger over there? My knee itches..."

"Sure Trenice – here..."

"Whew! Thanks..." I swung my leg up on the couch and kicked that bitch right in the stomach...

"Dammit!"

"Oh my God – I'm sorry Sissy – you ok? I swear – I hate this fuckin' cast – God I wish I listened to you Jordan – I'm really sorry Sissy," I lied with fake tears in my eyes for emphasis as I pretended to scratch my knee...

"That's ok Trenice – let me get up so you can stretch your leg."

Mission accomplished ... tee hee hee..."Thanks Sissy. Jordan hand me the pictures we got..." Jordan handed me the pictures looking perplexed as ever..."See this picture Grandma?"

"Yea? So?"

"So Jordan warned me not to lean over this bar here but would I listen? Nooooo – I just had to get the picture – So Jordan held on to me and I leaned over the bar and took the picture..."

"Trenice are you telling me you leaned over this bar? Where the falls are?"

"Yes Grandma."

Grandma popped Jordan upside the head as she said, "You stupid ass – she could've drowned!"

Grandma it wasn't his fault!"

"I don't give a damn whose fault it was Trenice! I swear if you put your brain in a bird, the damn bird would fly backwards! And Jordan why the hell didn't you tell her she was crazy?"

"I'm sorry Miss Gladys."

"You should be... wait a minute...how did you break your leg?"

"I leaned over the bar while Jordan was holding me and took the picture. When I tried to get back up I dropped the camera in the water so I leaned forward to get it..."

"Oh my God!" my mother screamed.

"That's when I slipped over the bar and fell in..." The fake ears were right on cue... "The only reason I didn't go over the falls and drown is 'cause my leg got caught between the rocks – Jordan was so scared he reached in and yanked me out as hard as he could..."

"Calm down Trenice – the important thing is that you're ok," Grandma said as she hugged me...

"Trenice?"

"Yes Grandma?"

"What did the paramedics say when they came to get you?" Jordan's eyes got wide as quarters again...

"We hobbled back to the hotel, we changed our clothes, and then Jordan drove me to the hospital."

"Why'd you do all that?"

"Well, besides being embarrassed for falling in, we could've gotten a big fine for attempting to go over the falls...they have signs all over the place..."

"Damn Trenice – no one can ever accuse you of living a dull life can they?" Sissy said.

Damn – maybe I shouldn't have kicked Sissy in her stomach – she feelin' all sorry for me 'n shit..."I guess not Sissy," I said with my head down...I added a few more fake tears for emphasis...

"Trenice?"

"Yea Aunt Trudy?"

"You sure that's what happened?"

"Trudy leave her alone!" Grandma said.

"But Ma..."

"Dammit Trudy I said leave her alone!"

"Stop it!" I screamed.

"Now see what you did Trudy? I told ya leave the damn girl alone!"

"Grandma she's not bothering me!" I screamed.

My mother just threw up her hands, shrugged her shoulders, and muttered, "I don't fuckin' believe this shit..." Little did they know I couldn't fuckin' believe this shit...

"What's wrong with you Claire?" Aunt Trudy asked.

"What's wrong with you Trudy? Trenice doesn't have to explain a fuckin' thing to you – and you gonna ask her if she's sure that's what happened – like she would make the shit up..."

"Well it is a little hard to believe Claire..."

"Go to hell Trudy..."

"That's enough you two..." Grandma said.

"See Ma – then you wonder why I don't come over here – everything revolves around your precious little Trenice – the perfect little angel that does no wrong..."

"Oh my God – stop it!" I screamed. "Aunt Trudy what the hell's the matter with you? You really think I would damn near drown myself to get some attention? I swear – I thought we were finished with this bullshit after what happened with Rosalind – damn!" No one said a word. I couldn't believe I actually said that shit!

"C'mon Sissy let's get the hell outta here," Aunt Trudy said as she went out the door. Sissy followed right behind her and let the door slam.

"Don't be slamming my damn door Sissy!" Grandma yelled. Now I was glad I kicked that bitch in the stomach!

"I'm sorry Grandma – this is all my fault."

"No it isn't either Trenice." My mother said. "I don't know what Trudy's problem is Ma – Trenice didn't do a damn thing to her and I sure as hell wasn't gonna sit here and let her call Trenice a liar!"

"No one's expecting you to do that Claire," Grandma said.

"Trenice I gotta get going," Jordan said as he headed towards the door...

"I'm going with you Jordan," I said.

"Trenice you got a cast all the way up your leg – you need to stay off it." Grandma said.

"Grandma we've been sitting for nearly 10 hours – I'll be ok – Jordan will make sure..."

"Oh right – like he made sure your ass didn't fall in the first place." Grandma said sarcastically.

"I'll be back later Grandma," I said as I damn near pushed Jordan out the door into the hallway..."

"I don't fuckin' believe this shit!" Jordan said.

"Hi Sissy!" I said deliberately loud so Jordan would know we weren't alone.

"Hi Trenice – be careful – you don't wanna break the other leg..."

I wanted to tell her shut the fuck up but I didn't..."I sure don't Sissy – see ya later."

"Ok – take care," she said as she went into her apartment and closed the door. "Damn – she bein' all nice 'n shit like she really feels sorry for me..."

"Maybe she does Trenice..." Jordan said.

"Yea right – let's get outta here before...bye Aunt Trudy..."

She walked past us and knocked on Sissy's door. When Sissy opened the door, Aunt Trudy went inside. Jordan sighed and said, "Let's go."

Soon as we got downstairs, as if things weren't bad enough, Tony opens the lobby door. "Hi Tony," I said.

"Hi Trenice – let me get the door for you."

"Good lookin'," Jordan said as we left the building. I was so glad we stopped to rent a car before we got to Grandma's house.

Once we got in the car Jordan asked, "So that's our story?"

"Yes."

"You sure about this?"

"Well we damn sure couldn't tell them the truth!"

"I can't believe they believed you – if I didn't know any better, I'da believed you too!"

"Yea I laid it on pretty thick – I even cried on cue," I laughed.

"Aunt Trudy almost blew yours wide open."

"She damn sure did – I couldn't believe that shit – and Grandma jumped in right on time too."

"You know we can never tell anyone the truth now Trenice."

"It'll be our secret."

"We can't even tell Jake and Rachel – and you sure as hell can't tell Char!"

"I know, I know!"

"You think we can pull this off?"

"We got past Grandma didn't we?"

"We're not outta the woods yet Trenice."

"I can repeat my performance again if I have too."

"Oh you will have too – believe me!"

We stopped at Jake and Rachel's house first. "Not again," they both said as we got outta the car. When we told them the 'story' they were both in shock.

"Oh my God – I would'a left the fuckin' camera in the water!" Rachel said.

"Man I know you was about to shit on yourself when Trenice fell in the falls," Jake said.

"That was nothing compared to Trenice's grandmother. She pooped me upside my head and told me I should'a told Trenice she was crazy!"

"Get the fuck outta here!" Jake said.

When we told them everything that happened Rachel said, "Maybe you should stay away from your Aunt Trudy – she's got some major issues."

"I wish I could Rachel – but Sissy lives right down the hall from Grandma."

"Damn – I forgot about that."

"Well gotta stop and see Char so we'll see ya later," Jordan said.

"Alright – we'll get up later," Jake said.

"That wasn't so bad," Jordan said as we got in the car."

"No it wasn't," I said.

"Trenice?"

"Yea?"

"This is kinda weird – but it's also kinda fun."

"Fun?"

"Yea – keeping our secret."

"Yea – it is kinda fun."

We sat for a moment then I said, "I wonder what Dr. Campton will think?"

"Depends on what you tell him."

"I'm gonna tell him the same thing I'm telling everyone else!"

"Ok, ok Trenice – calm down!"

"I'm sorry. Let's go see Char and get this over with."

"Okay."

When we got to Char's house she was looking out the window. She ran downstairs and came to an abrupt stop when she saw me. "Again Trenice?"

"No, no, no Char – it was nothing like that this time. Let's go upstairs and we'll tell ya what happened," Jordan said. When we got upstairs we told her the whole 'story.' She sat there for a few then she said,

"Yea right."

"Whatchu mean Char?"

"You can tell that story 1,000 times but we all know that's not what happened."

"Char, you think Trenice made this up?" Jordan asked.

"I know she did."

"What makes you say that?"

"Cause I know Trenice better than you think and I know damn well she ain't fall off no bar." Jordan and I looked at each other without saying a word. "So you broke another bed?"

"No Char."

"You sure?"

"Positive."

"Well if you don't wanna tell me that's ok – I'm your best friend – I've always been there for you and I've never betrayed you – you know you can trust me – but that's okay – don't tell me."

"Oh alright already – I fell but it wasn't over the bar – and that's all I'm gonna say." Jordan threw up his hands and looked at me, shaking his head...

"Trenice?"

"Yea?"

"You remember last year when I broke my leg?"

"Yea."

"How do you think I broke my leg?"

"I don't know – I never asked you…"

"What was I doing when I broke my leg?" I thought about it for a minute…

"Oh my God!" I screamed.

"Thaaats riigghht!"

"Char, you broke your leg the same way Trenice broke hers?"

"How else would I know she made it up?"

"I wonder if Aunt Trudy broke her leg too," I said.

"Why would you say that?"

"Char you wouldn't believe it. Trudy started trippin', Miss Gladys jumped in it, Claire and Trudy had words – I swear I don't know what her problem is."

"Jordan, Trudy's been acting like that ever since Trenice started living with her grandmother."

"You should've seen it Char – Claire cursed Trudy out and told her Trenice didn't have to explain a fuckin' thing to her – after it was all said and done she left and Sissy went right behind her and let the door slam!"

"What started all that?"

"She thinks I'm lyin' Char."

"Then Damn!"

"Grandma defended me along with my mother – and the thing that's so fucked up is I said I thought we were through with the bullshit after what happened with Rosalind!"

"Oh I know she ain't speakin' to you now!"

"She's not," I said.

"I swear – Trudy is so fuckin' immature – she just mad 'cause you said that shit!" Char said.

"I know Char."

"You think they believe you?"

"They do Char – even Sissy was feelin' sorry for me and bein' all nice 'n shit!"

"Damn Trenice – what you gonna do about Trudy?"

"It doesn't matter – everyone else believes me and I even showed them pictures to back up my story."

"Damn girl – you good!"

"Yea she's good alright – Grandma popped me upside my head and told me I should'a told Trenice she was crazy!" Jordan laughed.

"Damn Trenice – I hope she never finds out."

"Who the fuck's gonna tell her?" We all bust out laughing.

"Especially with Aunt Trudy on the case – I wouldn't be a bit surprised if she didn't try to call and check on your story," Char said.

"She can call if she wants – she won't get anything," I said.

"Well we gotta get goin' Char – you ready Trenice?"

"Yea – I'm ready."

"See you soon Char," Jordan said.

When we got to Jordan's house Miss April started right in…"I thought you were gonna stay away from the Holiday Inn?"

"Y'all never learn do ya," Miss June said as she laughed. We just shook our heads.

"Trenice you alright?" "Yea – I'm ok Miss April – Jordan was actually more afraid than I was."

"Why was Jordan afraid? What happened!"

"Can we sit down for a minute Mum-Mum?"

"Here Trenice – sit down," Miss April said as she pulled out the kitchen chair.

"Now what happened?" Miss June asked as she got up in my face closer than Sissy – damn!

"Jordan, get the pictures..." Thankfully it didn't take much to convince them – it's true what they say – a picture really is worth a thousand words!

"Mum-Mum we gonna go upstairs – we'll be back ok?"

"Alright Trenice – don't you fall down those stairs and break your other leg," Miss April said.

"Alright – I'll be careful," I said as we left to go upstairs.

When we got upstairs my mother answered the door.

"Hi Miss Claire," Jordan said as we went inside.

"Damn – again Trenice?" my mother said as everyone laughed and Marlowe shook his head back and forth.

"Mommy?"

"Yes Shaliyah?"

"Trenice isn't fat right?" Jordan and I looked at each other then at my mother, then back at Shaliyah.

"No she isn't Shaliyah – why do you ask?"

"And Jordan is big but he's not fat either right?"

"No Shaliyah – why?"

"So why do the beds keep breaking then?"

We couldn't hold it in any longer. Jordan and I were holding our stomachs along with everyone else – my mother dropped the frying pan on the floor and fell back into the table – we were all laughing so hard Shaliyah interrupted us...

"What's so funny? Why is everyone laughing at me?"

"We're not laughing at you Shaliyah – we're laughing at what you said."

"I don't get it – a broken bed is funny?" We were doubled over in laughter again...

"Stop laughing at me!"

"Jordan, get the picures..."

After we filled them in Shaliyah said, "Trenice?"

"Yes Shaliyah?"

"Can you sleep here from now on?" Everyone got real quiet.

"Shaliyah I live at Grandma's house."

"Mommy will let you come home – right Mommy?" Oh boy...

"Shaliyah, Trenice can come home anytime – she's always welcome here."

"Then why does she live with Grandma?"

"Shaliyah I live with Grandma because she will be all by herself if I don't live there."

"But we can go visit her then she won't be lonely. Aunt Trudy is there. Then you can sleep here and you won't get hurt anymore," she said with tears in her eyes.

"Well I can talk to Grandma about it but right now I need to stay there because of my leg."

"Why Trenice? Mommy can help you – right Mommy?"

"Of course Mommy can help me Shaliyah – but Mommy has more steps than Grandma."

"Oh so you gonna stay with Grandma so you can walk up the stairs?"

"Yes Shaliyah."

"Trenice?"

"Yes Shaliyah?"

"I think that's a good idea."

"You do?"

"Yea – Mommy is always yellin' at me to be careful 'cause I fall when I run up and down the stairs." We all started laughing again.

"Miss Claire I'm gonna take Trenice home now – we'll see you later."

"Oh ok – bye Trenice," she said as she gave me a kiss. "And please be careful."

"I will Mom."

"Trenice?"

"Yes?"

"I love you."

"I love you too – good night everyone!" Shaliyah damned near knocked me down when she ran up to me and hugged me tight.

"Take it easy Shaliyah – you almost knocked her down!"

"I'm sorry – you ok Trenice?"

"Of course I am silly – I'll see y'all tomorrow."

When we got back to Grandma's house she opened the door and said, "Both of you sit down here." Jordan looked at me and I shrugged my shoulders as if to say 'I don't know...' "The Quality Inn called." Shit, shit, shit, shit, shit! Jordan's eyes got wide as quarters but I remained cool...

"They did? Already?" Just then, Aunt Trudy and Sissy came walking in and sat down at the table with us – I wanted to knock their asses away from the table, but I knew damn well I couldn't do that...

"Yea – they said they wanted to talk to you about damages in the hotel room? What damages Trenice?" Aunt Trudy and Sissy were all in my face right along with Grandma. And she had that damned glare – the one that dared you to flinch let alone lie!

"I'm not sure – did they leave a number?"

"Trudy, give her the number." Aunt Trudy passed me the paper with a smirk on her face, but I had something for all of them. I picked up the phone and dialed the number and when they answered I asked for the management office.

"This is Trenice Robertson. Yes, that's right. Uh huh. Oh that's nice! Thank you very much!" When I hung up the phone they were all looking at me waiting to pounce..."Honey – guess what?"

"Umm... what Trenice?"

"Well remember when the toilet overflowed and they had to come in the room and replace the towels and stuff and you had to throw your jeans away?"

"Umm... yea... why?"

"Well everyone else that stayed on the same floor as us started complaining and threatened to take them to court – so they're sending us a certificate for a free weekend at the hotel and they're not charging us for the room!"

"They're not?"

"Nope – they wanted me to call them back so I could let them know if we wanted a check or if we wanted them to credit the credit card we used…isn't that great?"

"Yea – I guess it is," Jordan said. Grandma, Sissy, and Trudy just looked at me as if to say 'yea right' but they didn't say anything.

"Ma I gotta go – see ya tomorrow."

"Alright – bye Trudy, by Sissy."

"I gotta get going too – bye Miss Gladys."

"Good night Jordan," she said as she went down the hall.

After Jordan closed the door Grandma asked, "You want some coffee?"

"Sure Grandma." I sat at the table and watched my grandmother intently – I knew she was thinking and I knew she wanted to ask me something…

"Trenice?"

"Yes Grandma?"

"Never mind – here," she said as she placed the coffee on the table.

"Thanks Grandma."

Chapter 40

First thing I did when I got up was call Ms. Tyree in Payroll. I knew I had to brace myself...

"Again Trenice?"

"Ha ha ha...very funny."

"So how long will you be out?"

"I don't know for sure – I won't know until I go to the doctor."

"Ok – we'll put you out on disability – but make sure you have your doctor fax us a copy of the papers ASAP."

"Ok – will do."

"Trenice?"

"Yes?"

"Try not to break another bed while you're out," she laughed.

"Right now I'm in no condition to break anything – let alone another bed," I said matter-of-factly.

"Yea right Trenice," she laughed.

I hung up the phone and shook my head. "I don't think I'll ever live this down," I said to myself.

"Live what down Trenice?"

"Oh – good morning Grandma."

"Good morning."

"I was just on the phone with Ms. Tyree in payroll."

"Oh boy – I can imagine how that went," Grandma laughed. "She thinks you broke another bed doesn't she?"

"Everyone thinks I broke another bed Grandma."

"Did you?"

"Grandma!"

"Well?"

"Grandma I explained..."

"Trenice, just because I defended you doesn't mean I'm stupid."

"I never said you were stupid!"

"Don't get huffy with me Trenice!"

"Don't call me a liar and I won't get huffy!"

"I didn't exactly call you a liar Trenice..."

"You don't exactly believe me either!" I said as I slammed the door and hobbled down the stairs. When I got to the bottom of the stairs Tony was right there.

"Hi Trenice."

"Hi Tony."

"Let me get the door for you," he said as he opened the door.

"Thanks." Thank God the cab pulled up just as Sissy and Aunt Trudy were coming up the walkway. I got in the cab and slammed the door before they could speak to me – they probably weren't thinking about speaking to me anyway.

When I got to Jordan's house he was coming out the building.

"Can you wait here please?"

"Ok, but don't be too long – time is money."

I got out the cab and Jordan said, "What are you doing here?"

"You don't wanna see me? Fine then..."

"Trenice what's wrong with you?" he asked as he pulled me into a hug. "You know I wanna see you!"

"Can you come with me?"

"Sure." We both got in the cab and went to the Parkside Diner for brunch.

While we were at the table I explained what happened with Grandma.

"Well she's not stupid Trenice."

"Not you too – damn!"

"Calm down Trenice. I'm on your side, remember?"

"Yea sure," I said sarcastically.

"Why are you so mad anyway? If she knew the truth..."

"First of all she'll never know what really happened. Second of all we didn't break another bed, so I'm not lying when I tell her that!"

"Okay – okay," he laughed.

"What's so damn funny?"

"You are. Now hush up and kiss me silly," he said as he pulled me into a kiss...

"Mmm..."

"Isn't that better?"

"Much better."

"Ahem – are you ready to order?"

"Don't hate bitch," I said under my breath.

"Excuse me?"

"I said I'd like a western sandwich." Jordan looked at me giggling.

"And you?" she asked Jordan.

"I'll have pancakes and beef sausage."

"Would you like anything to drink?"

"Coffee for her, tea for me, and two glasses of water."

"Would you like lemon for your tea?"

"No – I'll take milk and sugar."

"I'll be back with your drinks."

"You are so bad," he said as she walked away.

"Fuck her," I laughed.

"What's gotten into you?"

"I dunno – I guess I'm frustrated 'cause of what happened earlier.

"Well the only way you can get away from that is if you move out," Jordan laughed. I looked at him without saying a word. When I sighed and put my hands under my chin he said, "Uh oh... what are you cooking up?" Just then the waitress came back with our drinks and put them on the table.

"Your food is coming right up."

"Thank you," we both said in unison.

While we were drinking our coffee and tea I said, "After we leave here I need to go see Dr. Campton."

"You do?"

"Yea – he's the one that has to take the cast off anyway."

"Oh I forgot about that... so are you gonna go back to your job when the cast comes off?"

"Probably – I like my job and the benefits are good so I don't see why not."

"Well I took this week off so I don't have to go back until Monday."

"What are you doing later today?" I asked as the waitress brought our food.

"Nothing – Why? You have something in mind?" He asked.

"You have to ask?"

When we left the diner we went straight to Dr. Campton's office. "I'm sorry but you don't have an appointment," the receptionist said.

"I know I don't (duh) but can you ask the doctor if he can squeeze me in?"

She sighed and mumbled under her breath, "I swear – this is sooo aggravating... hold on...Dr. Campton? Can you squeeze in Trenice Robertson? Ok... have a seat."

"Thank you." We didn't have to sit too long.

"C'mon in Trenice." When we got in the office he closed the door. "What happened this time Trenice?" Jordan and I looked at each other then at Dr. Campton.

"I fell Dr. Campton – but everyone else thinks we broke another bed."

"Well if I weren't a doctor I'd think that too."

"So you believe me?"

"Trenice I have your x-rays and I can tell by the break that you fell – you may have fallen out of a bed but you sure didn't break one," he laughed.

"Do you have a copy of the disability papers from my job?"

"No but we have papers here – we can just send them ours – as long as they're filled out properly you won't have a problem – do you still work at the Department of Social Services?"

"Yes."

"Ok – Jordan help Trenice up on the table so I can look at her cast." When I got up on the table he lifted up my leg. "See the x-ray there?"

"Yes."

"You broke your leg below the knee – the doctor put the cast on your leg over your knee so you can't bend it until it heals properly."

"Oh I see."

"He did a good job – we'll take care of everything as far as the paperwork – come back and see me in 6 weeks."

"Ok Dr. – thanks."

"Jordan?"

"Yes Dr.?"

"Make sure she's careful."

"Oh I will Dr."

When we got to the receptionist's desk I said sarcastically, "Excuse me – I need to **'MAKE AN APPOINTMENT'** for 6 weeks from today." She wrote the appointment down on a card and slammed it on the counter so hard she broke one of her nails...

"**DAMMITT!**" she yelled.

"Buh bye!" I said as we left.

"Trenice that was mean," Jordan laughed.

"Fuck her – that's what she gets for being nasty," I laughed.

"Trenice look at me," he said as he took my face in his hands. He held my face and as we looked into each other's eyes he said, "I wanna do more of this. I wanna do this every day. I wanna go to sleep with you. I wanna wake up with you. I wanna come home to you."

"Wow," I said with tears in my eyes.

"Let's get our own place Trenice." I pulled him close and kissed him so hard I startled him.

"Damn girl – is that a yes?"

"Yes! Yes! Yes!" When we left Jordan thought we were going home but he realized we weren't soon after we got in the cab. "Can you take us to 321 Main Street in White Plains?" I said to the driver.

"Ok Madam."

"Trenice what are you up to now?"

"You'll see…"

Chapter 41

When we got to Tyler's office Jordan was a little hesitant. "Trenice, are you sure about this?"

"Yes."

"Maybe we should leave well enough alone."

"Trust me."

"Ooookkkaaaayyyyy....."

"Hi Jordan, Trenice — Oh my God — what happened?" the receptionist asked as we walked into the waiting area.

"Oh I fell and broke my leg."

"Whew — for a second I thought you were suing another hotel," she laughed.

"So did everyone else," we laughed again.

"Do you need an appointment Trenice?" Tyler asked as he came out into the waiting area.

"Yes we do Tyler."

"Oh boy – c'mon into my office..." After we went into his office we closed the door and sat down.

"So what brings you both here?"

"Well, I fell and broke my leg while we were in Niagara Falls..."

"TRENICE!"

"Calm down honey...but that's not why we're here."

"Whew – glad to hear that at least.... go on..."

"Well, Jordan and I have decided to get a place of our own."

"Oh that's wonderful – congratulations!"

"Thank you."

"So when's the big day?"

"Oh we're not gettin' married."

"Oh sorry – I thought you were here to invite me to your wedding," he laughed.

"Oh you'll get an invitation to our wedding - don't worry – but that's not why we're here."

"Why are we here Trenice?" Jordan asked.

"Because we need Tyler to represent us."

"We do?"

"Yes."

"For what?"

"I'm tryin' to tell ya!"

"Okay – okay!"

"Go on Trenice," Tyler said.

"Well, as I said, we've decided to get our own place."

"Yes?"

"So since we have enough money for a down payment, we need you to represent us when we go to close on our new home."

"Trenice, that's a great idea and a great investment!"

"Trenice you never cease to amaze me, "Jordan said.

"So have you found anything yet?"

"No Tyler – we just decided to get our own place about an hour ago." Jordan and Tyler both bust out laughing.

"You don't waste any time do you?" Tyler asked.

"Not when it comes to something I want."

"Trenice are you sure we can afford a house right now? That's a big responsibility."

"Actually I was thinking more along the lines of a condo. They're more affordable and the monthly maintenance is cheaper than what we would pay in rent. Besides – unlike a co-op where you own shares in the building, with a condo, you own the apartment so you have more control."

"I see you've been doing your homework Trenice," Tyler laughed.

"Yes I have. "Well it would be my pleasure to represent you both."

"Okay – we'll keep in touch with you and let you know how everything's working out," I said as we left.

When we got outside Jordan asked, "How long have you been working on this?"

"I've been researching it since the day I met you," I said.

Jordan smiled, shook his head and asked, "So where to now?"

"Weichert Realtors." I said.

When we got to Weichert Realtors we signed up right away and I showed Jordan some of the properties I had been looking at. "Take this property for instance – they want $89,000 right?"

"Ok."

"It says the maintenance is $400 per month."

"Ok."

"It also says the taxes are $3,000 per year."

"Ok."

"So $80,000 over 30 years is $2,667 per year."

"Ok."

"So that's $222.25 per month plus $400 per month maintenance – that's $622.25 per month – without interest – I don't know how to factor that in."

"Ok."

"So $622.25 per month covers the mortgage and maintenance fees, $100 for the phone..."

"$100 for the phone?"

"I talk a lot remember?"

"Oh yea – go 'head..."

"Now where was I...oh yea...$100 for the phone, $100 for Con Ed, $100 for cable, $200 for food...more or less..."

"Ok."

"That's $1,100 per month for everything right?"

"Yea... except for one thing."

"What's that?"

"Well you said $80,000 – this is $89,000."

"Well in that example we offer them $80,000."

"Oh I see..." Jordan laughed.

"But you still haven't calculated the interest over 30 years."

"I have an explanation for that too."

"I bet you do," he laughed, "Go 'head."

"Well, we still have plenty of money from our suit right?"

"Yea?"

"So if we wanted this property we offer $80,000 cash – who wouldn't take that?"

"Ok."

"So when we close, there's little or no cost – we pay our attorney, the seller pays Weichert Realtors out of the $80,000, and we don't have to buy homeowner's insurance 'cause it's built into our monthly maintenance."

"So we just cut that $1,100 a month down to $900."

"Exactly – and we have plenty of money left over to furnish the condo."

"Well what if we want a property that costs more? Like $120,000 or $200,000?"

"If we want a property for $200,000 we can pay cash for it too – then we'll only have the maintenance and expenses – it's still a win-win 'cause we won't have a mortgage – just think of it that way."

"You have a point."

When we left Weichert Realtors we went to Char's house and I filled her in on the day's events.

"Trenice if you don't slow down you gonna break your other leg," she laughed. "You the only person I know that gets around more than anybody I know without a car – ha ha ha!"

"Very funny Char...besides now that Jordan and I are gettin' our own place...oops..." Jordan shook his head.

"I knew it," he laughed.

"You're what? When? Why? How?"

"As soon as possible, because we want to be together, and we're using the money we got!" I said as we all laughed.

"I'm happy for both of you," she said as she hugged me. "And I better get an invitation to the housewarming party."

"You won't need one since you're throwing it," I hollered.

"Them damn – thanks for telling me," she laughed. "I love you guys," she said as she hugged us both.

"We love you to Char – by the way – how's your friend?"

"Oh he's good girl – he was here earlier – we had breakfast then we had some dessert!" she hollered.

"Stop it – my stomach hurts!" I said. After we stopped laughing long enough to regain our composure I asked, "So Char – when am I gonna meet your friend?" She got quiet for a few minutes... "Char?"

"I might as well tell ya now..." she sighed.

"Tell me what Char?"

"He wants to wait until everything is final – he doesn't want anyone running back to his wife tellin' her shit. You probably think he's full of shit right?"

"Not at all."

"Really? Then what do you think?"

"I think if he never gave a damn about her and if he never had any respect for her he wouldn't care one way or the other. I also think he's being very considerate of her feelings and so are you – neither one of you are rubbing salt in the wound." Char started to cry.

"What's wrong? Did I say something to upset you?"

"I love you so much girl," she said as we hugged each other.

"I love you too Char."

"I need some advice."

"You do?" we both said in unison.

"Yea - his wife might be pregnant."

"Damn – perfect timing," I said sarcastically.

"That's what I said too. I don't know her to say she lyin' or nuthin' but she ain't say nuthin' 'bout bein' pregnant until after he filed for the legal separation."

"Damn Char."

"Now he talkin' 'bout he love me but he wanna be there for his child – so I asked him if he gonna go back to his wife and he said he don't know what to do – so where the fuck does that leave me?"

"Char, you can't blame the man for wanting to be there for his child," Jordan said.

"I understand that but if they're legally separated how the fuck is she pregnant? Either she pregnant by someone else or him – he need to go back to her 'cause I don't need this shit!"

"Wait a minute Char – did you ask him?" Jordan asked.

"Yea."

"What'd he say?"

"He said he's not."

"Well maybe he's telling the truth."

"And maybe he's lyin'," Char said.

"Char, don't get mad..." Jordan said.

"Ok."

"Why are you with him?" Jordan asked.

"That's a dumb question," Char said.

"Is it?"

"Whatchu mean?"

"Why are you with him?"

"'Cause I love him!"

"Ok – do you trust him?" Char hesitated.

"I don't know."

"Char you invested a lot of time in this relationship. You put up with..."

"I ain't put up with shit!" she interrupted.

"Let me finish. You knew he was married right?"

"Yea, yea, yea..."

"And you stayed with him anyway."

"I know, I know..."

"He got a legal separation from his wife right?"

"Yea."

"Char you gotta decide whether you trust him or not. Think about it from his point of view..."

"His point of view?"

"Yea. He's tryin' to do the right thing by both of you. He doesn't want to hurt you but he wants to be a father to his child and give him a Mom and Dad who will be there for him. If he doesn't think you trust him anymore you could wind up pushing him back to her."

"I never thought about it that way."

"You waited this long right?"

"Yea."

"So give him the benefit of the doubt – you'll both find out soon enough if she's pregnant or not."

"What if she is pregnant? I don't want to lose him."

"Maybe you should tell him that. He probably doesn't want to lose you either."

"You really think so?"

"Char – the man's been with you all this time and he got a legal separation from his wife so he could be with you – does that sound like he wants to lose you?"

Char jumped up from the table and nearly choked Jordan she hugged his neck so hard.

"Easy girl!" Jordan laughed. "Well we gotta get going – we got a few more stops to make," Jordan said.

"Call me later girl."

"Ok I will," I said as we went downstairs.

"That was really sweet of you," I said when we got downstairs and started walking. You gave her reason to hope again."

"Well I'm glad she's happy Trenice but to be honest, that's the last thing I was tryin' to do."

"I don't understand…"

"What don't you understand Trenice?"

"You were so nice…"

"Yes I was but she's in a bad situation all the way around. His wife has the clout – she has nothing – even if they wind up gettin' divorced and he marries Char – his wife gets the home, the alimony, and the child support."

"Damn – that's cold."

"That's reality."

"I'm glad you didn't tell her that."

"Trenice, I know you love Char and you don't want her hurt any more than I do – but she went into this with her eyes wide open."

"Yes she did but…"

"But nothing Trenice."

"So what's she supposed to do?"

"She's supposed to find her own man Trenice."

"I don't get it – why are you so mad?"

"I'm not mad Trenice. I love Char but why is she putting up with this shit?"

"But you said..."

"I know what I said Trenice – he doesn't want to lose her – but he may not want to lose his wife either."

"So why..."

"Why didn't I tell her all that?"

"Yea!"

"Would she have listened?"

"No."

"I hope everything works out the way she wants but divorce can be very ugly – especially when children are involved – and if his wife is pregnant..."

Jordan didn't say anything else for a good 5 minutes. As we walked side by side, I took his hand in mine. We continued walking hand in hand without saying anything for a block or so, and then I released Jordan's hand and moved in closer to him, wrapping my arm around his waist. He put his arm around my back, pulled me closer to him, and we continued to walk with our arms wrapped around each other until we got to Jake and Rachel's house.

Chapter 43

When we got to Jake and Rachel's house I let Jordan fill them in on the day's events.

"Wow – you two are finally gonna make that move," Jake said.

"Yes we are – I can't wait to wake up every day with Trenice," Jordan said as he pulled me close to him.

"Oh boy – I can see you two won't be able to keep your hands off each other," Rachel laughed.

"Shit – we don't keep our hands off each other now," Jordan laughed.

"We love living together don't we honey?" Jake asked as he looked at Rachel.

"Hell yea – come and go as we please, walk around the house anyway we like, stay in bed all day if we want..."

"I could get used to that," I said.

"Once you have it you'll never go back," Rachel said.

"I'll never want to go back," I said as I kissed Jordan. "If we end up half as happy as you two we'll be fine," I said.

"Aww... ain't that sweet honey?" Rachel asked as she lay in Jake's chest and he wrapped his arms around her.

"Yea – that's what I want for us," I thought to myself. "I can see it now – Friday night, Saturday night – we can play spades at our house!" I yelled.

"Yea – we can drink up your liquor, eat up your food, and throw up on your brand new couch," Rachel said matter-of-factly.

"Damn Rachel – I'm sorry."

"Girl please – you think you the only one that blessed someone's couch? I got drunk and threw up on my mother's butter-leather couch – we couldn't even clean it – she had to throw that $5,000 couch out."

"Oh my God – what happened?" I asked.

"You see where I'm livin' right?" We all hollered.

"Char told me she better get an invitation to the housewarming – I told her she won't need one since she's throwin' it...ha ha ha!"

"Girl you are too much!" Rachel said as we all laughed. "What did she say?"

"She said thanks for telling her!" I hollered as they all laughed along with me.

"Well I know she's happy to do it," Rachel said.

"Yes indeed." I said.

"Well it had to happen sooner or later," Jake said.

"You tell your Grandma and them yet Trenice?" Rachel asked.

"No Rachel – we just decided to do this today."

"Today? You've only been looking on line for a few months – how did you know?"

"I've been looking on line for years Rachel. I was just waiting for the one."

"Oh my God – you two are sickening!" Rachel said as we all laughed.

"Yea and we're sickening too," Jake said while tickling Rachel until she laughed so hard she turned purple.

"Well we gotta get goin' y'all – see ya later," Jordan said.

"Alright Jordan – keep us posted," Jake said.

When we got to Jordan's house, he filled his Mum-Mums in on the day's events.

"Well we know what to buy them don't we June?" Miss April laughed.

"Yea – a king size bed with a steel frame bolted to it so they can't break it... ha ha ha!" Miss June laughed. Miss April and Miss June laughed good and hard for a few minutes.

When they noticed we weren't laughing with them, Miss April said, "Uh oh...I think we hurt their itty bitty feelins..."

"Oh da poor babies," Miss June laughed. We just shook our heads.

"Have you told your Mom and Grandma Trenice?" Miss April asked.

"Not yet Miss April – we stopped here first."

"Well no time like the present," she said as she got up. When she opened the door we both looked at her funny. "Well? What are you waiting for? Let's go!" Miss June got up and Jordan held the door for us then locked it. We let them go in front of us...

When we got upstairs Miss April called my mother..."Claire? Claire! You home?" My mother opened the door and took a step back when she saw all of us.

"Hi April, June – c'mon in Jordan, Trenice." Jordan and I looked at each other and sat down. My older brothers and sisters came into the living room first then Shaliyah came in...

"Trenice!" she yelled as she jumped in my lap...

"Ouch!"

"Shaliyah I told you be careful!" my mother yelled.

"I'm sorry Mommy – you okay Trenice?"

"Yes – I'm fine Shaliyah – don't worry."

She got down from my lap, climbed up on Jordan's lap, put her arms around his neck, and lay down on his chest.

"Aww... ain't that sweet," they said as Jordan put his arms around her and hugged her back.

"So what brings you all here?" my mother asked.

"Well Claire, Trenice has a lot to tell ya," Miss April said.

"Well, what's going on Trenice?"

"Jordan and I are gettin' our own place."

"Wow – that was fast!"

"I guess."

"So when you movin' out?"

"I don't know yet."

"You tell Ma?"

"Not yet —I haven't been back since I left early this morning."

"Oh I heard all about this morning," she laughed.

"What about this morning Claire?" Miss June asked. Jordan and I just sat there with my brothers and sisters while the three of them laughed and joked about this morning, what they said downstairs, and whatever else they wanted to add.

"Trenice?"

"Yes Shaliyah?"

"Are you going far away?" she asked with tears in her eyes.

"Probably not."

"You're not?" she perked up.

"Shaliyah I'll never go too far away — how would you be able to come visit me?"

"Oh yeaaaa!"

"Well we gotta get going Ma — bye Miss April, Miss June," I said as I practically pushed Jordan out the door but I don't think they noticed — they had a bottle of 151 Bacardi on the table, the music was playing, and my mother yelled out, "Shaliyah, go git my cards off the night table!" as I closed the door.

Chapter 44

When we got home, naturally my two favorite people – Aunt Trudy and Sissy – were sitting outside on the bench with Grandma. I motioned for Jordan to sit down with me.

"Where ya'll come from?" Grandma asked as we sat down.

"We just left Mom's house."

"What's she up to?"

"They got a card game goin."

"Oh boy – what they celebratin'?"

"Jordan and I gettin' our own place."

"Oh? Since when?" My two favorite people were all ears and eyes – I wanted to smack em – damn!

"Since a few hours ago."

"Oh...I see. Well it was gonna happen sooner or later I guess."

"So when you leavin'?" Aunt Trudy jumped in.

"I don't know yet...why?"

"Just wondering."

"I know you still comin' to see your Grandma," Sissy said.

"And she can come see me too," I said.

"Trenice wherever you go it better not have more than two flights of stairs – you know I can't walk up all those stairs – that's why I don't go to your mother's house."

"I know Grandma...well I guess I better go upstairs and get ready for tomorrow," I hinted to Jordan.

"What's going on tomorrow?"

"I don't know yet Grandma – but I know I gotta get up early," I lied.

"C'mon Trenice – I'll walk you upstairs," Jordan said.

"Ok."

When we got upstairs and closed the door I pulled Jordan into a kiss which he was more than happy to oblige me with...

"I can't wait for us to go home..."

"Me too..."

"Well good night..."

"Good night..."

"I love you..."

"I love you too..."

Aunt Trudy pushed the door open so hard she cracked the wall with the door knob..."Dammit Trudy didn't I tell you to stop bangin' the door into the fuckin' wall?" Grandma yelled as they came in.

"Damn Ma – sorry." She was sorry alright – sorry she didn't catch us in the act.

Aunt Trudy and Sissy didn't stay long - thank God. After they left, Grandma went into the kitchen to make coffee. I was sitting at the table writing and when Grandma came out the kitchen she placed a cup of coffee in front of me, sat down at the table next to me, and peered over my shoulder. When I folded the paper so she couldn't read it she said, "Oh you writing a love letter?"

"Something like that."

"Oh ok – I guess I'll go on inside then…"

"Grandma?"

"Yes Trenice?"

"Thanks for the coffee."

"You're welcome," she said as she went down the hall.

When I finished writing, I went down the hall and knocked on Grandma's bedroom door.

"Yes?"

"Can I come in Grandma?"

"Sure." I sat down on the bed next to Grandma and let her read the song I wrote to Jordan:

For a Long Time

VS I   I met you once by chance. Infatuation grew. I knew right then and there I wanted you. You took me by surprise, such kindness in your eyes. I asked myself, "How long can this be true?"

Change 1   The answer was quite clear. I knew you were sincere. I felt that I would always have you near.

Chorus   For a long time. I'm sure we'll be together. For a long time. I know it lasts forever. For a long time. I look into your eyes and now I see. For a long time, it'll be you and me.

VS II   I know you now so well. You're happy – I can tell. I feel this is the happiest I've been. I love you oh so much. I need your loving touch. We have the kind of love that's hard to win.

Change 2   With promises we made, emotions never fade, and we are one as long as our love stays.

"I'm glad you're so happy Trenice."

"Me too Grandma."

"You have a lot of happiness ahead of you," she said as she hugged me.

"Good night Grandma."

"Good night Trenice."   As much as I was looking forward to being with Jordan, I got a little sad as I started missing Grandma already.

Chapter 45

I got up bright and early. I wanted to give Jordan the song I wrote. I sat at the kitchen table, waiting for the kettle to whistle, daydreaming about what it would be like gettin' up in the morning, making coffee, and cookin' breakfast, while Jordan was sitting at the table readin' the paper...

"Dammit Trenice will you turn that kettle off!"

"Oh! Sorry Grandma!" I yelled as I jumped up from the table and turned off the kettle...

"What the hell are you doin' in there that you couldn't hear the kettle anyway? You sleep?"

"Um...yea...I fell asleep..."

"Figures."

I called Jordan right away as I started making coffee...

"Hi sweetheart."

"Hey."

"Whatsa matter?"

"Oh nothing..." I giggled.

"What's so funny?"

"Well, I was sitting here day dreaming about you and I was so into it I didn't hear the kettle – Grandma asked me if I fell asleep...   hold on... - yea Grandma?"

"Are you makin' coffee?"

"Yea Grandma."

"Good."

"Sorry 'bout that," I laughed.

"So did you finish your breakfast?"

"No – Grandma woke me up hollerin' about the kettle," I laughed. "I'll be over in a little while ok? I got something for you."

"Ok – see you in a bit."

"I love you."

"I love you too."

I got up just in time...Grandma was on her way down the hall and when she came towards the kitchen I was holding two cups of coffee in my hands. I placed them both on the table and sat down.

"What – no breakfast?" she asked.

I bust out laughing.

"What's so damn funny?"

"Nothing – it's just that Jordan and I were just talking about breakfast."

"Oh so you havin' breakfast with him?"

"Probably."

"Oh ok – so whatchu have planned for today?"

"I dunno for sure – I guess I'll know when I go over there."

"You leavin' right now?"

"Yea."

"You comin' back tonight?"

"Far as I know I am."

"Jordan not workin' Trenice?"

"He took off this week – hes goin' back to work on Monday."

"Oh ok."

"See you later," I said as I gave her a kiss.

When I got to Jordan's house I gave him the song right away. "This is nice," he said as we kissed. We had been kissing for about 10 minutes when Miss April and Miss June interrupted...

"Ahem."

"Oh – good morning Mum-Mum."

"Good morning Miss April, Miss June."

"What brings you here so early?" Miss April asked.

"I had something for Jordan."

"Oh? Well where is it Jordan? Can we see it?"

"It's private."

"Oh it's a love letter?" Miss June asked.

"Something like that," Jordan said.

"Show'em honey."

"You don't mind?"

"No I don't mind."

"Oooookkkaaaayyyy....." Jordan said as he pulled the song out of his pocket.

"Oh this is nice – brings back memories," Miss April said.

"Yea?" Miss June and Jordan said in unison.

"Yea – your grandfather used to write me poems all the time – I still have some of them."

"Ma you never told me Dad used to write you poems," Miss June said.

"Yea – he gave me a different poem every day for the first month we were courting...some of them were so silly like red light green light 1, 2, 3 – I love you and you love me."

"Aww...that's sweet," I said.

"Oh I'll never forget this one – every time I see your face, I'm remember when we last embraced in our special place..." She got quiet as she sat and reminisced for a moment... "Those were the days," she said.

"I bet they were Ma," Miss June said.

"So what are you two up to today?" Miss April asked, changing the subject.

"I don't know yet Mum."

"Well I guess you'll fill us in on the details when you get back later."

"We will Mum-Mum – see ya later," he said as he gave them both a kiss.

"Bye Miss April, bye Miss June," I said as I hugged and kissed them both.

When we got downstairs Jordan said, "I think your song is really nice."

"You do?"

"Yea. I was thinking maybe we could stop at Cain's house and put it on tape...we can call William and invite him up also if that's ok."

"I love it! We haven't seen them since I broke my ankle!"

"Okay – let's go see if they're home then."

When we got to Cain's house he was all smiles and hugs. "How've you been? I haven't seen you all for weeks – come on in!" When he saw my leg he got real quiet. After we got inside he went and got a chair from the kitchen and propped my leg up on it as I sat down on the piano bench. "So did you break another bed?"

"What took you so long man?" Jordan laughed.

"Well I wasn't gonna ask but..."

"Man listen – everyone else asked," Jordan laughed again.

"So did you?"

"No," Jordan said.

"I fell and broke it when we were in Niagara Falls."

"Oh boy – I'm not even gonna ask what you were doin'," he laughed. Just then there was a knock at the door. "Le'me get that," Cain said as he got up to get the door. We heard the door close so we didn't think anyone was coming in, but when we looked up and saw William, we were surprised...

"William!" we both yelled in unison.

"Hey! Watchall doin' here?"

"We was just talkin' 'bout you man," Jordan said as they hugged.

"Man it's been a long time – oh my God – again Trenice?" We all bust out laughing.

"No, no, no – I fell when we were in Niagara Falls."

We spent an hour or so catching up – Cain told us how his children have grown and how they're doing in school, William told us how his oldest daughter moved out and it was just him and his wife at home, and we told them that we were gettin' ready to get our own place.

"Congratulations!" they both yelled in unison.

"When did you decide to do this?" Cain asked.

"Jordan asked me to move in with him a couple a days ago," I said.

"Well I wish you both the best," William said.

"Years from now the kids will move out and you'll be on your 2nd honeymoon," he said. Jordan and I looked at each other and smiled. We never talked about kids but we read each other's minds right then and there.

"I can't wait for my 2nd honeymoon," Cain said as his two youngest boys ran into the living room, both of them tripping over my leg — one landing in his daddy's lap and the other hitting the floor. They bust out laughing but their laughter was cut short —

"Didn't I tell you two stop running through the damn house!" he yelled as he smacked them both upside the head. They started to cry but he yelled after them, "Don't make me come in there and give you something to cry for!"

"I was gonna call you 'cause Trenice wrote another song and I wanted y'all to hear it," Jordan said, changing the subject.

"Oh yea? How does it go Trenice?" William asked. I sang the song for them and waited for Cain or William to tell me what they thought. Neither one of them said anything for a few minutes, then Cain went to the piano and started playing the melody, Jordan and William both started adlibbing, and I started singing again. We spent the next few hours putting my song to tape, taking breaks in between to eat everything from Italian wedges to potato chips to pizza to McDonalds to Kentucky Fried Chicken. It was just like the good old days when time passed and we didn't have a care in the world — and when Cain's kids came home from school that afternoon, they made a beeline for the kitchen 'cause when they saw all the boxes and bags, they knew there was plenty left for them.

Chapter 46

The phone rang at 9 a.m.

"Trenice?"

"Yes Grandma?"

"Telephone."

"Okay – I'm comin'," I said as I jumped out of bed and ran down the hall...

"Hello?"

"May I speak with Trenice please?"

"This is she."

"Hi Trenice – my name is Vanessa and I'm calling from Weichert."

"Hi Vanessa! Thanks for calling me back so quickly."

"I've gone over your application and we have everything we need –how soon are you looking to move?"

"As soon as possible."

"Are you homeless?"

"Not really – why do you ask?"

"Let me put it this way – if I found you something today and we could close within 30 days – would you be able to do that?"

"Definitely!"

"Oh ok – we're good to go then...what did you have in mind?"

"Well, Jordan and I are looking for at least two bedrooms..."

"Jordan? Jordan Williams?"

"Yes."

"Oh ok – so you two are buying this together."

"Yes."

"So you want at least two bedrooms – if I found you a 3 bedroom in your price range, would you be interested?"

"Definitely – actually, we'd prefer a 3 bedroom..."

"Ok – I'll keep that in mind – I have some co-ops and some condos available – do you know the difference between a co-op and a condo?"

"Yes - with a co-op you get a certificate for shares in the building – with a condo you own it – like a house."

"Basically that's it – would you be interested in a town house?"

"Sure."

"Okay then – if you like I could take you to see a 2 bedroom condo later this evening in your area – are you available at 6 p.m.?"

"Yes we're available."

"Ok – where shall I pick you up?"

"253 North Broadway, Yonkers, NY."

"Is that a private house?"

"No – it's an apartment building – but don't worry – we'll meet you outside."

"Ok – I'll see you at 6 p.m."

"Ok – thanks Vanessa."

"Who was that Trenice?" Grandma asked.

"That was Vanessa from Weichert."

"Weichert?"

"Yea – that's the realty agency we registered with."

"Oh – she found you an apartment already?"

"She has a few things in mind for us."

"Well make sure you read the fine print before you sign anything – you know sometimes you gotta pay 1 month's rent, 1 month's security, and one month's broker's fee equal to your rent."

"Oh I know Grandma."

"You're gonna need money for furniture too – that's another thing - what're you sleeping on?" She didn't wait for me to answer... "I guess you don't want your bed huh?" she laughed.

"My bed's too small for two Grandma," I laughed.

"So you gettin' a one bedroom?"

"Naa... we want a two or three bedroom."

"Why so many rooms? You're not pregnant are you?"

"Hell no! – Oh – sorry..."

"You want kids Trenice?"

"One day."

"Well it's gonna be hard enough to buy furniture for 3 rooms – let alone 5 or 6."

"I know... I guess I can't put furniture on my registry huh?" I laughed.

"You can try Trenice – you never know... but don't be surprised if the furniture stays on the registry though – especially since you have such expensive taste," she laughed.

"True...but I won't worry about it...we can do one room at a time..."

"Well, all you really need to start is a bed, a dresser, and a kitchen table. When people come over they can sit at the kitchen table until you get living room furniture – you can get that after you move in."

"One of my friends moved into her apartment and slept on the floor for a week."

"She slept on the floor Trenice?"

"Yea."

"Why she do that?"

"Well, she wanted brand new carpeting for her bedroom, but she didn't have enough money for new carpeting and a new bed, so she chose the carpeting," I laughed.

"So she went from sleeping in a bed to sleeping on the floor?"

"Yep – she said she didn't care 'cause it was 'her' floor."

"That does make a difference – nothing like having your own."

"Grandma you never wanted a house?"

"Naa...too many headaches – I don't have time for mowing the lawn, raking leaves, shoveling snow, emptying garbage..."

"You never wanted a co-op or a condo?"

"Not really...besides – I don't need a bunch a little ole ladies telling me what to do or how to do it..."

"How do they get on the committee anyway?"

"Most of them have lived there for so long they just nominate each other," she laughed.

"Sounds like this is gonna be fun," I laughed.

"Oh it'll be fun alright – running back and forth, moving, packing, unpacking – you'll have a blast," she laughed.

"Well I better call Jordan and let him know we have an appointment later," I said.

"Oh yea? What time?"

"6 p.m."

"Why so late?"

"Gives people a chance to get home from work."

"Oh ok – do you know where you're going yet?"

"No."

"She didn't give you an address?"

"No."

"How you gettin' there?"

"She's gonna pick us up at Jordan's house."

"Oh excuse me – back when I looked for an apartment you got the paper, made some phone calls, and got there on your own."

"Grandma we're not gettin' an apartment."

"Oh?"

"We're gonna get a co-op or a condo."

"You got money like that Trenice?"

"I can come up with a down payment," I lied.

"How you gonna do that?"

"I can apply for a loan through my credit union – you only need to have an account open for 30 days and have good credit."

"Don't you think you should do that first?"

"Oh I already did."

"You don't waste any time do you Trenice?"

"Well – if they were gonna turn me down I figured I might as well find out sooner rather than later..."

"How long you been working on this Trenice?"

"I started working on this right after I met Jordan," I laughed.

"Your mother's right – you are an astronaut.

"What makes you say that Grandma?"

"Most of us live in the present – you know – next week, next month – you project years into the future," she laughed.

"I remember when I was 9 years old – I told my mother when I grew up I was gonna have a big house with 6 dogs, 6 cats, and 6 kids – and they were all gonna have their own room," I laughed.

"Yep – you're an astronaut," she laughed.

"Well I better catch Jordan before he goes to lunch," I said as I picked up the phone.

"I'm surprised you're not running down there to have lunch with him."

"I probably would if I didn't have this cast on," I laughed.

"Hello?"

"Hi Honey!"

"Hey Beautiful."

"Vanessa's gonna pick us up in front of your house tonight at 6 p.m."

"Who's Vanessa?"

"She's from Weichert."

"Oh – that Vanessa...she found something for us already?"

"She thinks so," I laughed.

"What do you think?"

"She said she wants to take us to look at a 2-bedroom condo."

"Oh? Where is it?"

"I don't know – she said in our area."

"Oh boy – she didn't give you the address huh?"

"Nope."

"Okay – I'll see you tonight then."

"See you tonight."

"I love you."

"I love you too."

"Ma? Ma? Where you at?" Aunt Trudy yelled as she came in.

"I'm in the bathroom!"

"Oh sorry...hey Trenice," Aunt Trudy said as she closed the door behind them.

"Hi Aunt Trudy – hi Sissy."

"Hi," Sissy said as she sat down.

"Can't even take a shit in peace," Grandma said as she came down the hall..."

"Hey Miss Gladys," Sissy said.

"Hey Sissy – Trenice you makin' coffee?"

"I guess I am," I mumbled.

"What?"

"I said yea – I'm makin' coffee."

"Trenice when you goin' back to work?" Aunt Trudy asked.

"I'm not going back to work until after I get this cast off, Aunt Trudy."

"Trenice and Jordan are going to look at a place tonight," Grandma said.

"Damn – you found something that fast Trenice?"

"No Trudy – Vanessa is picking them up tonight to show them a place."

"Who's Vanessa?"

"She's the real estate agent."

I just continued making coffee without gettin' in the conversation – besides – they were doing just fine without me...

"I thought they only took you out to show you property when you want to buy something."

"They are buying, Trudy."

"For real? You and Jordan buying a house Trenice?"

"We might."

"Oh – excuse me," she laughed as I put the coffee down on the table and sat down with them.

"So you and Jordan got money like that huh?" Sissy asked.

"Fuckin' nosy bitch," I thought to myself, "I swear – I can't wait to get outta here..." "We'll come up with something," I said.

"So what are you lookin' for?"

"2 or 3 bedrooms."

"Why so many bedrooms? You're not pregnant are you?"

"No Sissy – I'm not pregnant – we just want more than 1 bedroom!" I snapped.

"Uh oh – somebody's in a mood today," Aunt Trudy laughed.

"I'll see you all later," I said as I finished my coffee and got up from the table. I went down the hall, jumped in the shower, got dressed and headed for the door...

"Where you goin'? Grandma asked.

"I'm goin' to Char's house Grandma – I'll be back later," I said as I closed the door. I could hear them all laughing as I walked down the hall and proceeded to hobble down the stairs. Naturally, as luck would have it, I ran right into Tony when I got to the bottom of the stairs...

"Hi Trenice."

"Hi Tony."

"Le'me get the door for you..."

"Thanks," I said as I hobbled out the door and down the hill.

Chapter 47

"Who is it?"

"It's me Char – open the door!"

"Wait a damn minute!"

"Never mind – I'll come back later," I said as I turned to leave.

"Girl, where you goin'?"

"I'm goin' back home I guess..."

"Trenice get in here," she said as she snatched me away from the steps and I toppled down on top of her. We bust out laughing as we hit the floor.

"That's what your ass get for pullin' on me in the first place," I laughed.

"Well you should'a waited for me to open the damn door," she laughed.

"Well you should'a opened it when I knocked the first time," I laughed.

"Well since you expect me to jump when you knock, le'me help you up," she laughed as she pulled me up off the floor.   "You alright?" she asked as we went inside and closed the door...

"Yea – I'm ok."

"You get around good on that cast."

"I'll be glad when I get this shit off too...

"Whatchu doin' here anyway?"

"Char?"

"What?"

"You busy?"

"I was..."

"Damn Char – I'm sorry! Why didn't you say something?"

"What was I supposed to say Trenice – I can't answer the door right now – I'm busy?"

"I bet that would've gone over well with your neighbors," I laughed.

"Well – I'm sorry Char – I could've come back later."

"It's okay – he had to leave for work anyway... so whatchu doin' here?"

"I got a call from Weichert this morning."

"Oh? Already?"

"Yea – she's pickin' us up tonight at 6 p.m. by Jordan's house."

"Oh wow – she thinks she found you something already?"

"Probably not."

"What makes you say that?"

"I don't want anything over there – I wanna move away – not around the corner or next door – it'll be like I never left."

"I hear ya."

"I can't wait to get outta there Char – they're startin' to get on my nerves – especially Sissy – nosy fuckin' bitch – I can't stand her ass!"

"What she do now?"

"Me and Grandma was talkin' before she and Aunt Trudy came over."

"About tonight?"

"Yea - so I told her me and Jordan was buying a co-op or a condo."

"Oh yea? You can do that?"

"Yea. So naturally, she had to tell Aunt Trudy and Sissy – not that it's a secret or anything – but here she come fuckin' askin' me why I want so many rooms – you not pregnant are you? I swear I can't stand that nosy bitch! Bad enough Grandma askin' me if I'm pregnant – did it ever occur to anybody that maybe we just want extra space? And if I'm pregnant it's not her fuckin' business anyway!"

Char just put a plate of scrambled eggs with bacon, home fries, and toast in front of me with a glass of orange juice and sat down. She started eating without saying a word.

"Char? Did you hear what I said?"

"Yea."

"That's all you have to say?"

"There's really nothing else to say Trenice. Sissy **IS** a nosy bitch. And they're gonna think you're moving so fast 'cause you're pregnant whether you are or not...my God – didn't they think you'd ever grow up?"

"I guess not Char."

"Well I'll be glad when you get your own Trenice – you and Jordan are gonna be so happy –

come and go as you please – sleep all day if you want…"

"I was wondering when you were gonna get around to that," I laughed.

"So when do you want your party?"

"Which one?"

"I'm only throwin' you one housewarming Trenice," she laughed.

"But Char – we gotta have a party too."

"We'll worry about partyin' after you move in," she laughed.

"Well Vanessa said once we find something, we can close in 30 days."

"Oh so you want your party as soon as you find something?"

"Actually, I was thinking I could have my housewarming party in my house."

"So you gonna wait until you get furniture and stuff?"

"I might…otherwise where would everything go? Grandma doesn't have the room and neither do you – unless I put ½ the stuff here and ½ the stuff at Grandma's house."

"What about your mother's house?"

"She got too many steps to be luggin' stuff from her house to someone else's" I laughed.

"So who you want me to invite?"

"The usual – I'm not inviting anyone from work – but I am gonna invite Tyler."

"You are?"

"Yea – and I'll invite Vanessa too."

"That's interesting – I wonder if other people invite their lawyers and their agents to their housewarming?"

"Probably."

"So what kind of food do you want?"

"I want a cake like the one they had at Linda's birthday party."

"Oh ok – that was good wasn't it?"

"Yea – butter cream frosting with vanilla pudding filling."

"It was good – I'll go order that soon as I find out when you're having it."

"Ok – make sure you invite Diedre & Carlos, Carolyn & Tim, Theresa & Joe, Jake & Rachel, Tish & Paul, Monique & Khoury, Roberta & James, Wanda & Mike, Bunny & Scott, Diana & Eric, Cain, William, and... oh yea – Tyler, and Vanessa."

"Trenice?"

"Yea?"

"How am I supposed to get invitations to all those people?"

"Give them to me – I'll pass them on – I know you don't see all of them."

"Oh ok – sounds good to me – you invitin' your Aunt Trudy?"

"No – I don't have to...she just shows up whenever there's a party," I laughed.

"She'll probably bring Sissy with her."

"Yea I know – but they'll be so many people there she can get in somebody else's business," I laughed.

"I know that's right," Char laughed.

"So tell me what you want and this way I can make sure everyone doesn't bring the same thing."

"Well, some stuff I don't care – like baked macaroni and cheese – they can bring as much of that as they want," I laughed.

"I know that's right – what else do you want?"

"I want lasagna, baked ziti, rice and beans, potato salad, fried chicken, collard greens, cabbage, sausage & peppers, fried whiting, Caesar salad, corn on the cob, and cornbread."

"Damn – oh wait a minute – I forgot – as much as we eat that might not be enough – ha ha ha!!"

"Now as far as drinks..."

"Drinks? What if everyone starts throwin' up all over your shit?"

"Oh they won't."

"What makes you so sure?"

"Cause I'm not buyin' living room furniture until after the housewarming."

"So where's everyone sitting?"

"Folding chairs."

"Smart."

"So as far as drinks, I want whatever they bring."

"Whatever they bring?"

"Yep."

"So what if everyone brings bottled water?"

"Then I really won't have anything to worry about – but as soon as I break out the cards, if there's no liquor here, someone will send out for some," I laughed.

"Yea – especially with Miss April and Miss June – they don't even need a reason to drink," Char laughed.

"I know – I remember when we first told them we were moving in together – you'd think they were buyin' a house the way they were celebrating," I laughed.

"So you want me to bring the cake – anything else?"

"Well…"

"What Trenice?"

"I wish you could bring your friend."

"Trenice don't start."

"Ok Char – I won't bring it up again – at least not today anyway – but if you chose to bring him, he's welcome."

"Well, I gotta get ready for work in a bit so call me later and let me know how things went."

"I will Char," I said as I got up to leave.

"Where you goin' now? You goin' back home?"

"Naa…I'm gonna stop at my mother's."

"Oh ok – see you later."

"Ok Char."

"Hi Miss April," I said as I entered the lobby."

"Hi Trenice – Jordan's at work."

"Oh I know – I'm meeting him here later tonight."

"Does he know you're gonna be here?"

"Yea."

"Y'all goin' out?" Miss June asked as she closed the door behind her.

"Yea – we're going to look at a condo."

"Y'all buyin' a condo?" they both said in unison.

"We're thinkin' about it."

"I guess you have a little bit more money than we thought," Miss April laughed.

"To be honest – it's the bank that has the money," I lied. "We just have to convince them to give it to us," I laughed.

"Good luck," Miss April laughed.

"Have a nice day."

"You too – we'll see ya later tonight," Miss April said as they left the building.

"Ma!"

"That you Trenice?"

"Yea."

"Oh ok," she said as she opened the door and waited for me to 'thunp' upstairs.

"I figured you'd be here sooner or later," she laughed.

"Whatchu mean by that?"

"I heard all about this morning Trenice."

"Figures."

"Whatchu mean by that?" she mocked.

"Nothing really. I just know that if I wanna be the one to tell you something I gotta tell you before they do," I laughed.

"You make way too much out of it Trenice."

"How – pray tell – do I do that?"

"You know they do it 'cause they know it bothers you – and they know it bothers you 'cause you let them know that – you get mad – they get a kick out of it – they do it again – you get mad again – they get a kick out of it again – the only way its gonna stop is if you put a stop to it."

"And again – I ask you – how – pray tell – do I do that?"

"Tell the bitch to mind her fuckin' business!"

"Ma! I can't tell Grandma that!"

"No you can't tell Ma that – but you can tell Sissy that!"

"But Ma – they were all there together…"

"Yea and when Sissy asked you if you were pregnant all you had to do was tell her that's none of her business..."

"Yea – and Grandma would've said knock it off Trenice... or don't be so rude Trenice."

"So then you knock it off – my point is you need to tell her mind her business. Once you start telling her that she'll think about it before she gets in your business again – or she'll ignore you and you'll have to tell her again – that's none of your business."

"You have a point Ma – like when they was all in my face when I called the hotel back – I swear I wanted to knock the shit outta her..."

"Wait a damn minute! What are you talking about?"

"Remember when we came back from Niagara Falls?"

"Yea."

"Well the hotel called and left a message for me about damages in the room."

"Damn Trenice – what the hell did you do up there? They suin' you?" I rolled my eyes and started tapping my fingers on the table..."Okay – I'm sorry – go ahead."

"So Grandma tells Aunt Trudy to give me the number – then they all sittin' there listening to my conversation."

"Ma tells Trudy to give you the phone number, then Ma, Trudy, and Sissy sittin' at the table all in your conversation? See that's what the fuck I'm talkin' about – that was none of her fuckin' business – Ma should'a gave you the message after they left – Trudy and Sissy didn't need to be all up in it – Ma keeps that shit goin' just as much as Trudy does!"

"I know – I heard them all laughing when I left too."

"See? I don't care what Ma or Trudy does – you don't owe Sissy a fuckin' thing – start tellin' that bitch to mind her fuckin' business!"

"Okay Ma – Ok!"

"That shit burns my ass...why you stay there and put up with that shit when you could've come back home is beyond me..."

"Ma you know damn well why I left home... and don't pretend like you don't..."

"What the fuck is that supposed to mean Trenice?"

"Oh boy... here we go with the amnesia..."

"Trenice don't you dare bring that shit up again..."

"Why Ma? What are you afraid of? Are you afraid you might find out you were wrong?"

"Me? Afraid? Of you? Don't make me laugh!" she hollered.

"Here we go with the amnesia..." I said as I shook my head...

"Dammit Trenice – stop it!"

"Stop what?" I said slyly.

"Look Trenice – why do we have to go through this every time you bring this shit up? If you have something to say – just say it dammit!"

"Okay then – I will say it!"

"Well it's about damn time!"

"What happened with Torbett was the straw that broke the camel's back..."

"Torbett? This is about Torbett?"

"No Ma – it's about you!"

"Oh I gotta hear this one..."

"I was the responsible one. I was the one that made the honor roll in school. I was the one that came straight home and made sure the house was clean so when you came home I could see that smile on your face. I did that 'cause I knew it made you happy Ma," I said with tears in my eyes.

"Yes you did Trenice. You were so proud of yourself. You used to say, "Mommy, close your eyes," and I'd close them each time even though I knew what the surprise was."

"Dad would be spillin' his liquor 'n shit all over the table, then he'd get mad 'cause I got an attitude and I'd wipe it up − sometimes he did the shit on purpose and I'd catch him laughing when I went back towards the kitchen − but most of the time he was drunk. I didn't care as long as he was quiet − but then all hell would break lose soon as you came home − he'd find somethin' wrong, ya'll start fightin' − Shaliyah start screamin' − we'd have to jump in and take hits ourselves just to keep him from hitting you..."

"I know Trenice − I know − why are you re-hashing all this?"

"Ma? Shut up... please."

"Ok − go 'head."

"When I met Torbett we were inseparable."

"No amnesia there..."

"Ma!"

"Alright Trenice − I'm sorry − go 'head."

"I know you didn't like him but I loved him."

"Yes you did Trenice."

"You put him down every chance you got..."

"I saw the same traits in him that your father has − I wanted more for you Trenice."

"Okay Ma – I'll give you that – but there's no excuse for what happened when you came home and saw Torbett in the house."

"I told you not to have him in my house when I wasn't home Trenice."

"And I tried to tell you I didn't have him in the house when you weren't home Ma – but noooo – you had to come in with guns blazin' talkin' 'bout, oh I know this bitch not fuckin' in my house!"

"Trenice your dad said that…"

"Yes he did – and you went right along with him Ma – you didn't say shit when he told Torbett get the fuck outta my house – he snatched Torbett by the arm and threw him out and you didn't even try to stop him – all those times I jumped in between you and Dad to keep him from beating on you – and the one time I needed you to defend me you didn't!" I screamed.

"First of all, if he hadn't been in the house when we weren't home it wouldn't have happened. Second of all, how was I supposed to stop your father from throwing Torbett out when I couldn't even stop your father from beating on me?"

"I'm not saying you were supposed to snatch him off Torbett Ma – but you could have at least tried to calm Dad down."

"Trenice you could have gone somewhere else – then you wouldn't have gotten caught."

"The only way I would have gotten 'caught,' as you put it, is if I was doin' somethin' I had no business doin' – which I wasn't."

"C'mon Trenice…what did you expect?"

"Ma that was 4 years ago – I just told you I wasn't doin' somethin' I had no business doin' – you didn't trust me then and you don't trust me now – and you wonder why I left."

"Trenice don't put all that on me – you were gonna be with Torbett no matter what anybody said – besides, look how everything turned out..."

"Yea Ma – look how everything turned out! I went to Grandma's house – and she believed me. And I never came back home.

"Trenice – you know damn well you could've come back home if you wanted too."

"Yea Ma – I could've – if I wanted too – but that's just it Ma – you hurt me so bad I didn't want too... see?"

"Oh I see just fine Trenice."

"Do you see Ma? Do you see what drove me away in the 1st place? Do you see why I went to Grandma's house? Do you see why I wouldn't come back here even when things didn't work out with Torbett? Especially with Dad still in the house?"

"I see a lot more than you think Trenice – believe me. Grandma kept her feelings to herself about Torbett so it only made sense for you to run to her. You didn't come back home 'cause you didn't wanna here I told you so."

"I don't believe this shit!"

"What's wrong Trenice? I was right all along huh," she laughed.

"She never told you..."

"Never told me what Trenice?"

"Grandma never told you what happened?"

"Oh I know what happened Trenice."

"No you don't – but you would've if you'da listened to me..."

"What was I supposed to do Trenice?"

"You were supposed to do what Grandma did."

"I was supposed to do what Ma did? What the fuck did Ma do that I should've done?"

"You were supposed to ask me what the fuck he was doin' in your house when you weren't home and I would've told you!"

"Fine Trenice - if that's what it's gonna take for us to finally be done with this ok – what the fuck was Torbett doin' in my house when I wasn't home?"

"Finally! After all this time," I whispered with tears in my eyes... "I was doing as I usually do – like I've done since grade school – cleaning the house so when you and Dad got home I could see that smile on your face when you came in the door. When I heard Torbett knock on the door I thought it was you and Dad so I unlocked it and went back in the kitchen to finish cooking. I had no idea Torbett was in the house until he tapped me on the shoulder. When I turned around and saw it was Torbett, I screamed...

"Scared you huh?" He laughed.

"Hell yea," I laughed as we hugged and kissed each other.

"Cmere you little sneak," I laughed as I saw Shaliyah peakin' around the corner.

"Don't be mad at her Trenice – I told her I had a surprise for you so she let me in," he said as he dropped down on one knee and opened the jewelry box.

"Will you marry me Trenice?"

"Uh Huh!" Shaliyah said as she peeked around the corner from the living room.

"Shaliyah, I think he was talking to me," I whispered with tears in my eyes as I looked at Torbett kneeling down in front of me with the ring.

"Well? Will you marry me Trenice?" he asked again with tears in his eyes...

"Yes Torbett – Yes – I'll marry you!"

"Oh yea!" Shaliyah yelled as she jumped up and down while Torbett put the ring on my finger.

"Where's Mom? Where's Dad?"

"I thought they were knockin' at the door but it was you," I laughed as we went into the living room and sat down on the couch.

"I can't wait to ask your Dad for your hand in marriage," he said as he kissed my hand.

"Good luck," I laughed.

"Doesn't matter what they say Trenice – you already said yes," he said as he kissed me.

"Yes I did, Yes I'll marry you!"

"Ahem!"

"Yes?" We both laughed as Shaliyah interrupted our kissing...

"Torbett this ring is beautiful – I had no idea..."

"I'm surprised Shaliyah didn't tell you..."

"Shaliyah? You mean to tell me you knew all this time and you didn't tell me? You little sneak – cmere!" I yelled as I grabbed her and tickled her.

"He made me promise Trenice," she laughed.

"I guess you really can keep a secret," I laughed.

"Yes she can," Torbett said as he grabbed her and we all hugged.

"How long did Shaliyah have to keep this a secret?"

"Not long – only since yesterday."

"Yesterday? You bought this yesterday?"

"Yep.   Shaliyah   saw   me   comin'   outta Woodrow's – she was so excited I thought she was gonna run home and tell you so I told her I promise not to tell that she was in the square when she was supposed to go straight home if she promised not to spoil your surprise," he laughed.

"Oh that was good – she would've kept the secret for a week at least," I laughed.

"Trenice?"

"Yes Shaliyah?"

"You won't tell right?"

"No Shaliyah – I won't tell – I promise."

"Ok."

"That's about the time you and Dad were on your   way   upstairs   and   you   started   calling me...Trenice? Trenice you up there?"

"Oh   shit – here they come – Shaliyah go inside..."

"Okay Trenice..."

"Yea Ma – I'm here!"

"Open the door – these bags are heavy!"

"Ok Ma – hang on..." and that's when I opened the door, you and Dad came in, and all hell broke lose," I said as I sat there and cried.

"Oh my God Trenice – I'm sorry – I had no idea – Ma never told me," she said as she put her arms around me to comfort me. "I can't believe you kept this inside you for so long..."

"I can't believe I never forgave you for something you didn't even know about..."

"I can't believe Ma didn't tell me – that should've been the happiest night of your life – that's alright though – I'ma let Ma have it the next time I speak to her..."

"Don't bother."

"Oh yes the hell I am Trenice – Ma had no business..."

"Ma let it go!"

"Excuse me? Let it go? You've been holding this inside you for the last 4 years – you couldn't forgive me – Ma knew all along – and you wanna just let it go?"

"Ma I thought you knew all along – now I know better."

"So do I Trenice – I don't give a damn what you say – I'ma let Ma have it the next time I talk to her..."

"I think I liked it better when I thought you knew all along," I sighed.

"Trenice I don't get it – all this time – why don't you want me to say anything to Ma?"

"It's not that I don't want you to say anything to Grandma – it's just....never mind..."

"Trenice stop it!"

"Stop what?"

"We've done this for the last 4 years – enough is enough!"

"You're right. I'm sorry."

"No I'm sorry – and Ma will be too when I get finished giving her a piece of my mind... Trenice?"

"Yes?"

"Does Trudy know?"

"Poor Shaliyah..." I sighed as I tried to avoid the question.

"Shaliyah?"

"Yea Ma – remember Shaliyah? She was there when Torbett bought the ring – she was so happy for me – you should've seen her peeking out from behind the doorway when I accepted Torbett's proposal – she was so cute..."

"Poor thing – she probably hates me as much as you do," she said between tears...

"I never said I hated you Ma."

"No but you said you couldn't forgive me..."

"Well I couldn't forgive you – but I didn't say I'd never forgive you..."

"I'm sorry Trenice..."

"I'm sorry too Ma..."

"What are you sorry for?"

"I don't really know what the hell I'm sorry for," I laughed.

"Poor Shaliyah – she's been through so much – we must'a scared the shit outta her..."

"She's a lot stronger than you know Ma..."

"She's a lot like you Trenice – she kept this to herself..."

"I can't believe she never talked about it – not even to me..."

"She probably blames me 'cause you never came back home..."

"Probably..."

"God I wish I had just asked you what the fuck he was doin' in my house...," she sighed. We sat there for a few moments and then my mother bust out laughing.

"What's so funny?"

"Well..." she laughed, "I was just thinking..." she laughed again, "I'll know better next time..." she hollered.

"There isn't going to be a next time!" we hollered in unison.

"Oh well, we might as well stop cryin'," I laughed.

"Might as well," my mother laughed. We stopped hugging and sat there at the kitchen table for a few minutes and just looked around the kitchen. We didn't say anything to each other, but neither one of us tried to move away from the table. After about five minutes of silence, I got up from the table. My mother looked up at me to see if I was leaving, but I could see the relief in her face when I opened the cabinet and took down 2 cups. I saw her smiling as I looked through the cabinets until I found the coffee. I put the tea kettle on and she continued smiling as I looked on the shelves in the refrigerator until I found the half & half. As I pulled the sugar down out of the cabinet, the kettle started whistling so I turned the kettle off, made two cups of coffee, sat them on the table, and sat back down with my mother.

"So do you wanna know what happened at the hotel?" I asked as we started sippin' on our coffee...

"Sure – you can tell me what happened at the hotel – but you need to answer my question first."

"What question Ma?"

"Oh it's like that? Ok then – be like that - I already know the answer anyway."

"Ma!"

"Never mind Trenice – let's get back to what happened at the hotel - I'm not stupid – so what happened?"

"Oh my God – le'me find out – Grandma didn't tell you? I actually get to tell you something?"

"Trenice will you tell me already!"

"Ok – ok. When we were in the hotel the toilet backed up and our room got flooded so Jordan had to throw away some of his clothes. Everyone else that was on the same line we were had the same problem – somebody threatened to sue – so the hotel offered us a certificate for a free weekend at the hotel and they gave us a credit – they didn't charge us for the weekend."

"That's it?"

"Yea Ma – why?"

"Girl please – I don't give a damn about that – I wanna know how you really broke your leg," she hollered.

"Oh… no you don't…"

"Oh…yes I do…"

"Oh…no you don't…"

"You're right – maybe I don't wanna know… so where you goin' tonight?"

"Vanessa's picking us up to go show us a condo."

"Where?"

"She said it's in our area."

"Oh boy…"

"That's what Jordan says."

"Well you don't have to take the 1st thing you look at."

"I know… but beggars can't be too choosy."

"I know you can't afford a mansion but you can get something nice too."

"I know Ma."

"So how many rooms you lookin' for?"

"At least a two bedroom – it would be nice if we could get 3 bedrooms."

"You stand a better chance of gettin' a 3 bedroom co-op in your price range than a condo."

"Really Ma?"

"Yea - condo's are more expensive but the maintenance is lower – co-ops are cheaper but the maintenance is higher – but you might get lucky – see what...what's her name?"

"Vanessa."

"See what Vanessa says – she's gonna find you something 'cause she wants to get paid."

"True. I'm surprised you didn't ask me if I was pregnant too."

"Why? 'Cause you want 2 or 3 bedrooms?"

"Yea."

"First of all – I'm your mother – I'd know if you were pregnant – and 2nd of all – common sense tells you – you don't buy a 1 bedroom anything unless you plan on livin' alone the rest of your life."

"Thank you."

"So you're having a house warming right?"

"Yea."

"Where you havin' it? Char's house?"

"No – mine."

"You're having your house warming after you move in?"

"Yea."

"Why?"

"Well this way, we don't have to carry stuff from place to place – we'll just have it put away 'cause it'll already be in the house."

"Where's everybody sitting Trenice?"

"Foldin' chairs."

"Trenice you can't do that."

"Why not?"

"We have too many people in this family – they won't all fit in folding chairs unless you have a room big enough to hold 50 people."

"50 people? I ain't invitin' 50 people."

"You don't have to – once people find out there's free food they'll come."

"Oh it's not free."

"Trenice – don't tell me you're charging people..."

"No Ma!"

"Oh – whew!"

"It's everybody bring a bottle and a dish."

"Everybody?"

"Yea."

"So you want everyone to make something and buy you something too?"

"Yea – well family anyway."

"Oh ok – sounds like a plan."

"Well Char thinks it's a great idea..."

"I bet she does - she won't have to have all of us in her house," she laughed.

"It'll be better this way Ma – we need all the money we can get to furnish the place..."

"True... so what do you want me to bring?"

"Hmm...you make everything so good Ma – I dunno – you pick..."

"Ok – I'll bring baked macaroni and cheese."

"Ok – I'll let Char know – she's keeping a list."

"Ok good – I'll bring 2 pans so tell her no one else needs to bring it."

"Ok."

"So what do you need?"

"Everything Ma."

"Tell ya what – I'll buy you that sectional you fell in love with last week...that'll be my gift to both of you."

"I love you Ma!" I yelled as I damn near knocked her out of the chair I grabbed her so hard.

"Easy girl!" she laughed.

"And Grandma said my furniture would probably stay on the registry..."

"You told Ma you were putting furniture on the registry?"

"Yea – why?"

"I hear ya Trenice – I'm buying you the sectional – who knows what else you'll get," she laughed. "I'll buy it as soon as you do the registry so it will be delivered to your new home right before the house warming."

"Thanks Ma. I'm leaving the plastic on it too – I don't want anybody spillin' shit on my couch!"

"Damn girl – you ain't even got it yet and you already talkin' 'bout people spillin' shit," she laughed.

"Mommy – open the door!" Shaliyah yelled.

"All you had to do was knock Shaliyah," she said as she opened the door.

"I did Mommy – but you didn't hear me 'cause you was talkin' to... Trenice!"

"Hey Shaliyah – how's my favorite girl?" I asked as she jumped in my lap and threw her arms around my neck.

"You stayin' here for a while?"

"Yea."

"Good," she said as she skipped down the hall to her room.

"Hi Trenice, Hi Ma," my brother Marlowe said as he came in.

"Ahem!"

"What?"

"Where's my hug?"

"My bad," he said as he hugged me and picked me up out the kitchen chair.

"Marlowe put me down," I laughed.

"Yea – put her down and give me my hug," my mother said with her arms outstretched.

"Can I have a hug too?"

"Of course," Marlowe laughed as he picked Shaliyah up, hugged her, and tickled her.

"How've you been Trenice?"

"I've been busy."

"Cast don't stop nothin' huh?"

"No it doesn't," I laughed.

"All right you two..."

"What'd we say?" we laughed in unison.

"Never mind," my mother said as Shaliyah looked back and forth between us.

"So how long you gonna be here Trenice?"

"Until Jordan gets home from work – then we're goin' out."

"You goin' to the movies Trenice?" Shaliyah asked.

"No Shaliyah – we're going to look at a place – if we like it we might buy it."

"Can I come?"

"Not this time Shaliyah...but you can come to the housewarming."

"Oh yea... Trenice?"

"Yes?"

"What's a housewarming?"

"When you get a new house or apartment, people come to your house to congratulate you and they bring you gifts for your new home."

"Oh so you gonna have a house party?"

We all bust out laughing.

"What's so funny?"

"Nothing Shaliyah – that's cute."

"Oh."

"Ma's buying me a living room set."

"Oh that's nice – I don't know what I'm gonna get you yet – but you need everything so I can't go wrong," Marlowe laughed.

"I know what I'm gonna buy Trenice," Shaliyah said.

"What Shaliyah?" my Mother asked.

"It's a surprise."

"Shaliyah that's ok – you don't have to buy me anything."

"Yes I do – right Mommy?"

"Yes Shaliyah."

"See – I told ya I had to buy you something Trenice."

"Yes you did Shaliyah."

"I'm gonna buy it tomorrow when I come home from school."

"Ok – but make sure you're careful crossing the street."

"I cross the street by myself every day – right Mommy?"

"Yes, but Trenice is right – you have to be careful crossing the streets in the square."

"I'm not going to the square Mommy – I'm going to the store you always send me to."

"You goin' to the store on the corner? Right where you get off the school bus?"

"Yea – that one."

"Ohh... ok..."

"I bet you can't guess what I'm buying you Trenice."

"You're right Shaliyah...I can't."

"Tee hee hee..."

"I'm sure I'll love it – whatever it is."

"I'll give you a hint..."

"Ok."

"Everybody needs one."

"Ooohhh... that's a tough one..."

"Give up?"

"Yea – but don't tell me ok?"

"Oh I'm not."

"Well I know I'm not buying you the same thing 'cause I'm not buying nothin' from the corner store – Shaliyah's probably the only one buying you something from the corner store," Marlowe said.

"I bet she ain't."

"What makes you say that Trenice?" Marlowe asked.

"Ma who always buys koolaid?"

We all bust out laughing.

"Girl you ain't right," my mother laughed, holding her stomach.

"I can hear her now talkin' 'bout girllll... you know you gotsta have koolaid 'cause everybody don't drink!" Marlowe laughed, holding his stomach.

"Yea – she be all up in your cabinet talkin' 'bout where da picher? Then she be all up in your freezer talkin' 'bout ain't ya got ice?" I laughed.

"Uh huh – and she pull out a can of sugar and makes the koolaid taste like syrup," Shaliyah laughed. We all bust out laughing again.

"Shaliyah how you know who we talkin' about?"

"Miss Birdie always makes koolaid for us when we go to Grandma's house," Shaliyah laughed.

Chapter 49

"Claire?"

"Yea?" my mother yelled as she got up to open the door.

"Trenice up there?"

"Yea she still here."

"Tell her Jordan's waiting downstairs with Vanessa."

"I'm coming down now Miss April," I yelled as I got up to go downstairs.

"Trenice you be careful on that leg – they can wait a minute..."

"I will Ma," I said as I hobbled to the door.

"Marlowe get the door for Trenice before she trips and breaks her other leg," my mother laughed.

"I'll get it!" Shaliyah yelled and tripped over Marlowe's leg as she tried to beat him to the door...

"You alright Shaliyah?" I laughed.

"Yea I'm ok Trenice," she said as she stood up and stormed back into her room. "Stop laughing at me!" she yelled.

"Damn – I didn't think she could hear us – that's fucked up," I said.

"Trenice she'll get over it – go on downstairs before Jordan comes up here after you," my mother laughed as she hugged me.

"Hmm... I kinda like the sound of that..." I said.

"First your ankle, now your leg – don't you think you should quit while you're ahead?"

"Bye Ma," I laughed as I closed the door behind me .

"Hey Beautiful," Jordan said as he kissed me.

"Hmm... I told my mother I like the sound of this," I said as I kissed him back...

"Y'all comin' or what?" Miss April yelled.

"We on our way now Mum-Mum," Jordan laughed as we went downstairs. Miss April and Miss June just laughed and shook their heads as we went past them down the stairs and out the door.

"Hi – you must be Trenice – I'm Vanessa," she said as she extended her hand. "Oh my goodness – what happened to your leg?"
Jordan and I looked at each other and bust out laughing.

"Was it something I said?"
We laughed even harder.

"Well I'm glad you're laughing – I could use a laugh too – let a sista in on a joke," she said.

"Long story," I laughed.

"We got a few minutes – give me the short version," she laughed as we got into her car. I was so glad she couldn't see Jordan rolling his eyes...

"So where are we going tonight Vanessa?"

"I found something on Ravine Avenue you might be interested in."

"Ravine Avenue?" Jordan asked.

"Yea – you know where that is?"

"Yea – I used to ball over there," Jordan said.

"This is right off of Point Street," she said.

"Down the hill from Rappaport Cleaners?" I asked.

"Yea – it's right down here," she said as she turned the corner and parked at the bottom of the hill. I could see the look on Jordan's face as he got out the car and I couldn't blame him. We were kinda relieved when we saw the complex wasn't directly on Ravine. As we went up to the walkway we saw another couple in front of us.

"I wonder if they're here to look the same place we are honey."

"Maybe."

"Let's follow them inside," Vanessa said as they got buzzed in. Just as I thought, they were going to the same place we were going to.

"Hi – come on in, the gentlemen said to us as we all went inside. Jordan and I stayed in the living room with Vanessa while the other couple went towards the bedroom. I like this color honey – it will go good with the sectional my mother's buying us."

"Your mother's buying the sectional you went to look at last week?" Jordan asked excitedly.

"Yup."

"Wow – that's nice."

"We had a long talk earlier today – she said since I liked it so much she would buy it for me," I laughed.

"Sounds like a nice Mom," Vanessa said. "So you like this color?"

"Yea – the sectional is navy blue with yellow and green pillows so the yellow will bring it out nicely," I said.

"Come look at the kitchen and tell me what you think," Vanessa said as I followed her into the kitchen. "I like the blue marble counter top – look honey – isn't this nice?"

"Yea it's nice – the kitchen's kinda small though," Jordan said.

"Yea, it is kinda small – but look at the dining area here," I said as I pointed to the dining area.

"Big enough for a table," Jordan said. "Can we keep the dishwasher?" he asked.

"Yes – the dishwasher's included," Vanessa said.

"How much is he asking?" I asked.

"He's asking $90,000." Jordan and I looked at each other but didn't say anything. Vanessa must have read our minds... "I can't tell you what you should offer or what I think of the asking price – I can only tell him if you're interested or if you wanna make him an offer."

"Oh... honey, let's go check out the bathroom and the bedrooms," I said.

"Ok – follow me," Vanessa said as we started down the hall. Jordan and I looked at each other and back at Vanessa when we got to the end of the hall. Neither of us said anything but I knew Vanessa had the same question on her mind that we did... "Here's the bathroom," she said as she opened the door and backed away from the bathroom rather quickly.

"C'mon honey – let's look in the bathroom," I said as I started to go inside and quickly backed away.

"What's wrong?" Jordan asked.

"Nothing – it's kinda small so I was just moving out your way," I lied. Jordan got to the doorway of the bathroom, peeked inside for about a minute, and backed away too.

"Yea – it is kinda small – is this the main bedroom over here?"

"Yes it is," Vanessa said as she showed us into the bedroom.

"How my man gonna take a dump while we in the kitchen? He should've waited 'till we left – damn!"

"Well honey maybe he had to go," I laughed. Vanessa didn't say anything but she wanted to laugh too. "Did he just leave?" I asked as we heard the door close.

"No that was the other couple leaving," Vanessa said as I opened the closet door.

"Well at least there's plenty of closet space," I said.

"Yea there is – let's look in the other bedroom," Jordan said as we walked down the hall towards the other bedroom. "I was wondering why he ran past us holding his pants," Jordan laughed. Vanessa couldn't hold it in any longer - she bust out laughing right along with me.

"Is he coming?" I asked.

"No he went back in the kitchen," she said as she showed us the closet.

"Well I guess we can go now," I said as we walked down the hallway towards the living room.

"Thanks – it was nice meeting you," I said as I extended my hand.

"Thanks for coming by," he said as he shook my hand.

"I'll be in touch," Vanessa said as we went outside.

"Damn I hope he didn't hear us," I said when we got downstairs.

"Oh well – like Jordan said – he should've waited until we left – he didn't even have the courtesy to spray," Vanessa laughed.

"We didn't give him time – he heard us comin' and had to jump up and run holding his pants up," Jordan laughed.

"So are you interested in making an offer?" Vanessa asked.

"No – it's too small," I said.

"Yea it is kinda small – I hope he can sell it but he may have to come down off that price," Jordan said.

"Well I can't tell you what you should offer – but you're not interested so it doesn't matter anyway – besides, I have something else I'd like to show you – I'll call you sometime next week," she said as she pulled up in front of Grandma's building.

"Ok Vanessa – good night," Jordan said as he got out the car.

"Good night Jordan, Trenice – see you next week," she said as I got out.

"Good night Vanessa," I said, waiving as she drove off.

Chapter 50

We went inside and started upstairs. That's when we heard all the commotion...

"I don't give a shit what you say Ma - you could've told me!"

"Claire, if you really wanted to know, you would've asked Trenice yourself," Grandma said.

"You are so full of shit and you know it Ma - you just wanted to gloat!"

"Claire you just mad 'cause Ma knew all this time and you didn't - that's what you get," Aunt Trudy said.

"Bitch shut the fuck up - ain't nobody talkin' to you!" my mother yelled.

Jordan whispered, "What's going on?"

"I'll fill you in later," I said as we continued to listen on the steps...

"Who you callin' a bitch?" Aunt Trudy said.

"You! Bitch!" my mother yelled.

"I said knock it off Claire!" Grandma yelled.

"No I will not knock it off Ma - I don't give a shit what you or Trudy says - you knew damn well when Trenice came here that night what the hell happened and you could've told me - you don't have a problem runnin' shit back and forth any other time!"

"What's she talkin' about Trenice?" Jordan asked.

"Ssshh!" I said as we continued to listen.

"You know what Claire - you can get the fuck outta my house!"

"Why you come in here talkin' to Miss Gladys like that anyway?" Sissy asked. Oh boy... what'd she go and do that for...

"Bitch, mind your fuckin' business! That's what the fuck your problem is now - I ain't Trenice - I'll bust your fuckin' ass!"

"Claire I told you get the fuck outta my house!" Grandma yelled.

"I got the fuck outta your house years ago Ma - you ain't said nuthin' then and you ain't sayin' shit now!" my mother yelled.

"Claire I'm not gonna sit here and let you talk to Ma like that," Aunt Trudy said.

"And I'm not gonna sit here and put up with this shit from you, Ma, or Sissy - you wanna sit here and act like you hollier than thow, you got Sissy all up in Trenice's business - and Ma - you ain't no fuckin' better - you keep the shit goin' and you be laughin' right along with them - I don't give a damn if I'm not welcome in your house - I told Trenice I was gonna come over here and tell you about yourself whether she liked it or not..."

"Trenice? What's Trenice got to do with this?" Grandma interrupted.

"Trenice told me everything that happend that night Ma - something you should've done a long time ago!" my mother yelled.

"Trenice ain't got shit to do with how you discrespectin' Miss Gladys," Sissy said.

"Bitch didn't I tell you mind your fuckin' business?" Once we heard the rumbling we knew what was going on...

"Get the fuck off me bitch!" Sissy yelled. Jordan and I were laughing with our hands over our mouths as we could tell that my mother was choking her...

"Trudy, get the fuck off me!" my mother yelled.

"Trenice come back..." Jordan tried to stop me but I was in the door already...

"Get the fuck off my mother!" I yelled as I snatched Aunt Trudy by the back of the shirt...

"Bitch please," Aunt Trudy said as she pushed me to the floor...

"Bang!"

Everyone stopped in their tracks. Jordan was standing in the doorway with his eyes and mouth wide open. Sissy was sitting on the couch with her eyes and mouth wide open. My mother and Aunt Trudy stood toe to toe looking at each other and then they both looked into the kitchen. I looked at Jordan, I looked at Sissy then I looked at my mother and Aunt Trudy. Nobody moved so I got up off the floor and went into the kitchen. Grandma was holding the gun in her hand and she had it pointed up at the ceiling. I stood in the doorway of the kitchen and looked Grandma in the eye for a few seconds but I didn't say anything. My mother and Aunt Trudy walked up behind me and stopped at the doorway.

"Grandma?" I asked softly.

"What?" she snapped.

"Um... you want a cup of coffee?"

"Do I look like I want some fuckin' coffee Trenice?"

"Um... no, but I figured since I was gonna make some... if you wanted a cup..."

"Move," she said as she pushed us out of the doorway and stormed down the hallway towards her bedroom with the gun in her hand. Jordan and I stood there and watched as my mother followed her down the hallway.

"I'ma go," Sissy said as she got up. Jordan opened the door and I moved out her way but Sissy wouldn't go out the door.

"Well?" Jordan said.

"I know you ain't throwin' nobody out my mother's house," Aunt Trudy said.

"Bitch please," I said.

"Shut the fuck up Trenice!" Aunt Trudy said.

"Oh I see I gotta come the fuck back out there 'cause I still got some damn fools up in here," my grandmother said as she came back down the hall with the gun in her hand...

"Fuck this," Aunt Trudy said as she went towards the door, pushed Sissy out, went out the door, and slammed it behind her.

"I swear she got one more time to slam my fuckin' door and I'ma slam her fuckin' head," Grandma said as she sat at the table. "Trenice?"

"Yes Grandma?"

"Where's the coffee?"

"Oh - I'ma make it right now - Ma you want some?"

"Might as well have some," she sighed as she sat at the table with my grandmother.

"Bitch ain't nobody beggin' you to have a cup of coffee with your mother - you can get the fuck outta my house!" Grandma yelled.

"How many times you gonna tell me that before you realize I ain't payin' you no damn mind," my mother laughed. Jordan and I started laughing too. We laughed for a couple of minutes until...

"Bang!" as Grandma banged the gun on the table.

"Trenice?"

"Yes Grandma?"

"Put this shit away," she laughed as she tried to hand me the gun...

"Oh hell no!" I laughed.

"Girl it ain't loaded," she laughed as she tried to hand it to me again.

"I don't care - I'm not touchin' it," I laughed as I put 3 cups of coffee on the table.

"Miss Gladys... you shootin' blanks?"

"You ever play Russian Roulette?" she laughed as she put the gun down on the table and started drinking her coffee.

Jordan sat down at the table with us and said, "No I haven't - and I'm not planning to any time soon," he laughed as we drank our coffee.

"Jordan you ain't drinkin'?" Grandma asked.

"You got Pepsi?"

"You waitin' on me to get it for you?"

"Oh no - I'll get it," he laughed as he got up from the table and went into the kitchen.

"So how did everything go today Trenice?" my mother asked, changing the subject.

"How much time you got?" I laughed.

"Oh I gotta hear this," Grandma said.

"Wait – le'me get my soda first," Jordan laughed.

When he sat back down at the table we both filled them in on the day's events. My grandmother was holding her stomach she was laughing so hard.

"Damn - he should'a took a shit before you got there," she laughed.

"That's what we said," I laughed.

"I can just picture him running out of the bathroom holding up his pants," my mother laughed.

"Reminds me of when Trudy used to sneak her boyfriend in her room from the terrace and I came home early one day and caught him buck as naked in her room," Grandma laughed.

"You lyin'!" Jordan laughed.

"You see she has a gun," my mother laughed.

"He damn near shit on himself," Grandma laughed.

"Miss Gladys you didn't!" Jordan yelled.

"I told him, "Muthafucka if I **EVER** catch you up in my house again I'll blow your fuckin' head off," my grandmother laughed. "He snatched his clothes and climbed down the terrace holding his pants!" my grandmother yelled as we all continued to laugh good and hard.

"Well Ma, I'ma get the fuck outta your house now," my mother laughed.

"Fuck you Claire," Grandma laughed as they hugged each other.

"Jordan you leavin' yet?" Grandma asked.

"Yea – Trenice you wanna take a walk with me?"

"Sure," I said as I got up to walk out the door.

"I'll walk out with you," my mother said as we went towards the door.

"Trenice, you comin' back tonight?" Grandma asked.

"Yes Grandma – I'll be back tonight."

"Don't be too late – I ain't stayin' up all night ya know," she said as she closed the door.

"I won't Grandma!" I yelled as we started down the stairs.

Naturally, as luck would have it, when we got outside, we ran smack into Aunt Trudy and Sissy. I thought I was gonna be able to hold it together until we got down the street but once my mother started laughing, I couldn't hold it in any longer. Jordan couldn't either...

"Ah ha ha ha ha ha ha ha ha ha... "

"Ah ha ha ha ha ha ha ha ha ha... "

"Ah ha ha ha ha ha ha ha ha ha... "

"What's so fuckin' funny?" Aunt Trudy snapped. We just kept walking and laughing until we got about 2 blocks away.

"Ma I was ok until you started laughing," I said.

"I couldn't help it," she laughed.

"I can't believe this shit," Jordan laughed. "I don't know what the hell I'm laughing at," he said.

"Well I know what the fuck I'm laughing at and I don't give a damn who doesn't like it," my mother said. "I just hope Trenice doesn't get any shit behind it.

"Me to Ma, but if Aunt Trudy has her way..."

"All you gotta do is throw her boyfriend in her face – that'll shut her ass up quick," my mother laughed.

"I bet it will," Jordan laughed.

"Y'all goin' back to Jordan's house Trenice?"

"I dunno – are we Jordan?" I asked.

"No – let's go to the park," he said.

"Alright then – I'll see you again soon – good night," she said as she hugged us both.

"Good night Mom," I said.

"Good night Miss Claire," Jordan said.

"Jordan?"

"Yes Miss Claire?"

"You're gonna make a fine son-in-law," my mother said as she turned the corner and we continued toward the park.

When we got to the park Jordan didn't waste any time...

"Trenice?"

"Yes?"

"What happened?"

"Upstairs?" I asked, trying to avoid the real question.

"Yea."

"Well, actually that's normal," I laughed.

"That was crazy! How long Grandma been packin'?"

"I dunno."

"Oh so you knew she had a gun?"

"Yea - she used to keep it down at the Black Horse back in the day."

"I hope she never had to use it," Jordan laughed.

"I don't think so - I think they used the bouncers more than she used that gun - she probably had it in case someone was stupid enough to try and rob them," I laughed.

"I can't believe she actually fired it."

"You didn't have anything to worry about - she keeps blanks."

"How you know that?"

"She used to always say, "Good thing I keep blanks - be just my damn luck I'll shoot a muthafucka and wind up killin' em," I laughed.

"Well you all sure stopped in your tracks when she fired it."

"We had to."

"Why?"

"Shit you didn't see that look on her face?"

"Yea she was mad."

"Yea - Aunt Trudy will say, "Claire had no business comin' over here startin' her shit - if she had'a stayed her ass home none of this would'a happened..."

"Trudy always been like that?"

"Yea."

"That was some funny shit - your mother told Sissy, "I ain't Trenice - I'll bust your fuckin' ass!" Jordan laughed.

"That was some shit - I can't believe she tried to choke her," I laughed.

"Trenice?"

"Yes?"

"Why was your mother so mad anyway? Really?"

"Well when I went to talk to her earlier I told her about how I got a message from the Quality Inn and how Grandma had Aunt Trudy give me the number and Sissy was sittin' right there and they were all up in it while I was on the phone."

"And that's why she was so mad?"

"Hell yea! You should've heard her Jordan - she was yellin' tellin' me I didn't owe the bitch nuthin' and I need to start tellin' Sissy to mind her fuckin' business!"

"Damn! She got mad like that?"

"Hell yea! She even said Grandma keeps the shit going just as much as they do and they do it because they know it pisses me off and they laugh! She said Grandma had no business puttin' them in that and she should've waited until after they left to give me the message. Then she had the nerve to say she doesn't understand why I stay there and put up with that shit when I could've gone back home."

"I agree with Mom there."

"Me too."

"But there was something else Trenice... your mother's never been that mad - not since I've know her... and she wasn't leaving until she made sure Grandma heard what she had to say."

"I know. Turns out I was holding a grudge against my mother for nearly 4 years for something she didn't even know about. We really went at it and I accused her of having amnesia and she accused me of not coming back home because I didn't want to hear her say she told me so when Torbett and I broke up for good. Once I realized she really had no idea what happened that night I told her I could forgive her. She was really mad because we could've moved past this a long time ago. I told her to let it go but she wasn't listening to me or anyone else. She said we've been doing this for 4 years and enough was enough!"

"Trenice?"

"Yes?"

"What happened... that night? Did someone hurt you?"

"No... Not really..."

"So what happened then?"

"Well you know how I felt about Torbett."

"No I don't. How did you feel about him?"

"I really loved him Jordan."

"Ok."

"We met in high school and we were inseparable. My mother couldn't stand him – she put him down every chance she got."

"Maybe she saw something in him Trenice."

"Yea – that's what she said. But I think she should have let me see it for myself."

"Sometimes love is blind. Remember Rosalind?"

"Point taken."

"So go ahead and finishing telling me what happened."

"I told her they should've given me the benefit of the doubt and just asked me what he was doing in the house but instead, my dad comes in yelling about I know this bitch ain't fuckin' in my house – then he snatched him by the arm and threw him out."

"Damn. What she say?"

"She said if I have something to say I should fuckin' say it so I told her how I felt because she didn't believe me then. Even today - nearly 4 years later - all she could do was tell me that I had no business having him in her house when she wasn't home then I wouldn't have gotten caught. That's when I screamed at her and told her she could have tried to defend me for all those times I took licks for her but then she asked me how was she supposed to do that when she couldn't even stop Dad from beating on her."

"Damn Trenice – that's fucked up."

"Yea well the truth hurts sometimes."

"I mean that's fucked up that you let him hit you so he wouldn't hit your mother," Jordan said.

"It wasn't just me Jordan – it was all of us – Shaliyah included."

"Shaliyah?" She's just a baby.

"I know."

"So then what happened?"

"I told her all she had to do was do what Grandma did."

"What did Grandma do Trenice?"

"Grandma asked me what the fuck Torbett was doing in the house. So I told her."

"Well I wish you'd tell me."

"That's what I'm doing!"

"Ok – go ahead."

"Well my mother finally got around to asking me what Torbett was doing in the house. I had been waiting for that for so long I burst into tears."

"Damn Trenice." Jordan said as he pulled me close to him and put his arm around me.

"I was cleaning the house so when they got home I could see them smile. When I heard Torbett knock on the door I thought it was them so I unlocked the door and went back in the kitchen to finish cooking. I had no idea Torbett was in the house until he tapped me on the shoulder. When I turned around and saw it was Torbett, I screamed. He laughed 'cause he knew he scared me. I saw Shaliyah peakin' around the corner but he told me not to be mad at her because he had a surprise for me. That's when he proposed."

"He asked you to marry him?"

"Yup."

"Did you say yes?"

"Shaliyah said yes before I could," I laughed.

"But you said you'd marry him.

"Yes."

"So what happened after that?"

"He asked where Mom and Dad was. He wanted to ask my Dad for my hand in marriage.

"Wow. He's a real romantic."

"So while we're waiting for Mom and Dad he starts telling me that Shaliyah caught him in the square coming out of Woodrows so he promised not to tell she didn't go straight home if she promised not to ruin my surprise."

"Shaliyah kept the secret?"

"Yea – she only had to keep it for 2 days," I laughed.

"So what happened when your parents came home?"

"I heard my mother calling me in the hallway so I went out in the hall to help her with the groceries... they came inside, saw Torbett, my dad blew up, threw him out, and the rest is history."

"Damn Trenice. I'm sorry."

"So was I."

"That was supposed to be the happiest night of your life."

"Yea – that's what my mother said."

"How old were you Trenice?"

"When I met Torbett? In high school?"

"No – when he proposed."

"I was 20."

"Damn! I see why you left your mother's house!"

"Unfortunately, so does Shaliyah."

"Shaliyah?"

"Yea. I heard her crying later that night. My mother thinks she has issues because she used to see my father hit her all the time but I know for a fact that Shaliyah is angry at my mother for what happened. That's why she always asks me if I'm comin' back home."

"Yea – she almost cried when you said you were moving away."

"I know. I told my mother Shaliyah probably blames her for what happened that night too."

"You did?"

"Yes I did. Shaliyah never talked about it either. Not even to me."

"She didn't?"

"Nope. I think she'll be ok now though."

"What makes you so sure?"

"Well my mother and I always had some kind of relationship and Shaliyah and I are very close – plus, she sees how happy I am with you."

"So you mean to tell me your grandmother and your Aunt Trudy knew all this time and neither one of them said anything to your mother?"

"Nope."

"And all this time you thought your mother knew and didn't give a damn."

"Yup"

"I don't blame your mother for being mad. I'm surprised you didn't want her to say anything."

"I didn't want her to say anything because I knew what would happen - but now I'm glad the shit happened - Sissy needed to have the shit choked out of her," I laughed.

"Why didn't you tell me?"

"I dunno."

"Still hurt's doesn't it?"

"Actually, no."

"You sure?"

"Yea."

"So did Torbett leave you after that?"

"No. I left my mother's house and moved in with him. Everything was going good and we planned to get married but...."

"But what?"

"He lost his job. Then he started going out drinking every night, coming in 2-3 a.m. the next day. Then that damn fool hit me and thought he was gonna get away with it," I laughed.

"Oh my God Trenice? What happened!"

"I left. I packed my shit and went straight to Grandma's house. Been there ever since."

"He didn't come after you?"

"Yea, he did."

"So what happened?"

"We got back together for a minute. He used to come see me on the weekends for a while. Then it was every other weekend. Then it was once a month. Then I called him and told him it was over and don't bother me anymore."

"What did he say?"

"He said ok, then he hung up."

"No he didn't!"

"Yes he did."

"Wow. I can't believe this shit. This has been one hell of a day."

"And just think what would have happened if I listened to Aunt Trudy and just broke up with you."

"Oh that was **never, ever, ever,** gonna happen," Jordan laughed.

"Pretty sure of yourself ain't ya?" I laughed as he pulled me into a kiss.

"Oh yea," he said as he kissed me.

We hadn't heard from Vanessa since we went to see the property on Ravine Avenue and I was growing tired of waiting to hear from her. I'd been surfing on the Weichert for a few days and I nearly jumped out of my chair when I saw the following:

MOVE RIGHT IN TODAY! PACK YOUR BAGS AND MOVE RIGHT IN! RARE GEM 3 BEDROOM CONDO, 1.5 BATHS, PARKING, WASHER/DRYER INCLUDED, NEW APPLIANCES, PETS ARE ALLOWED! JACUZZI IN MASTER BATHROOM PLUS STORAGE LOCKER IS $42 PER MONTH.

Price: $321,000
Taxes: $2,902
Maintenance: $600

I immediately went to view the photo gallery. The living room, dining room, eat in kitchen, half bathroom, and washer/dryer closet were all on the left side near the front entrance of the condo. French doors led to the deck which faced the Hudson River and was in the back of the living room. The 2nd bedroom, 3rd bedroom, and master bedroom suite with a full bathroom & Jacuzzi were down the hall on the right side of the condo.

"Ohhh... we need to see this!" I yelled as I printed the flyer.

"Need to see what?" Grandma asked as she popped her head in my room...

"Oh... Poltergeist II is coming out," I lied as I pulled up the mortgage calculator and put in the figures...

Purchase Price: $321,000
Taxes: $2,902
Down Payment: $200,000
Mortgage: A little over $1,000 plus $600 Maintenance

"Oh... I thought you found another condo," she said as I folded the flyer and put it in my pocket...

"Nope," I lied again...

"I'm surprised you're not on the phone with that agent of yours – I figured you'd be a pain in her ass tryin' to get the hell outta here after what happened last week," she laughed.

"That's not a bad idea," I laughed. "I think I'll give her a call later today," I said as I printed out the calculations, folded the paper, and put it in my pocket.

"If you'd stop printing out your emails and go pick up the damn phone you just might get outta here sooner," she snapped as she went down the hall.

"Oooohhhhkkaaaayyy then...," I said as I turned off the computer, got up, and headed towards the door...

"Where the hell you goin' now?" she snapped.

"I'm going out – I'll be back later," I said as I closed the door behind me, went downstairs, and headed out the building past Aunt Trudy and Sissy without looking back, and headed straight for my mother's house.

"Who is it?" my mother snapped as I knocked on the door.

"Never mind," I said as I started to go back downstairs.

"Trenice get your ass in here," she laughed as she opened the door. "What's wrong with you today?" she asked as I went into the kitchen and took down two cups, turned on the kettle, and sat down at the kitchen table.

"Nothing..." I sighed.

"I thought we were finished with this bullshit," she said as she joined me at the table.

"Oh shut up Ma," I laughed.

"So what's wrong?"

"Nothing."

"Oh so you came over here for nothing?"

"I can't just come see my mother and have coffee? Something has to be wrong? Damn!"

"Now I see why Ma wants to knock the shit outta you sometimes," she laughed.

"The feelin's mutual," I said.

"I was just kiddin' Trenice," she said as the kettle started whistlin'."

"Hmph... I wasn't," I said as she made us coffee.

"Oh so you wanna knock the shit outta your grandmother – but nothing's wrong," she laughed.

"I don't wanna knock the shit outta anybody Ma – Grandma just has a bug up her ass today that's all," I said as I sipped my coffee.

"I thought you said nothing's wrong," she laughed.

"Can I use the phone?" I asked, completely ignoring her comment.

"Trenice, you don't need to ask permission to use the phone – but I am curious as to why you came all the way over here to use the phone when Ma has a phone," she laughed.

"Cause I know if I use your phone I won't have to explain shit to everyone else," I said matter-of-factly.

"You start tellin' people to mind their fuckin' business like I told you to and you wouldn't have to explain shit to anyone either," she laughed.

"Why go through all that when I can just come here, have a cup of coffee, and no drama," I laughed.

"Trenice you're welcome here anytime and you're welcome to use the phone, but you shouldn't have to come over here to avoid drama," she said as I picked up the phone and called Weichert, completely ignoring her comments.

"May I speak to Vanessa please? This is Trenice Robertson."

My mother listened intently to my end of the conversation...

"Hi Vanessa... I'm good... Yes... I know... Yes I found something and I'd like to know if it's still available... yes it's in Yonkers... ok... hang on... Ma, can you give me that pen over there... thanks... the listing number is MLS2437... Yes that's the one... We can see it tonight... ok... let me write this down... 600 North Broadway... 6:00 p.m.... ok... great... I'll let Jordan know... ok... see you tonight..."

"600 North Broadway? Isn't that where those nice condos are?" my mother asked.

"Yup."

"You goin' to look at a condo over there?"

"Yup."

"Those are kinda pricey – you sure you can afford it?"

"Yup," I said as I showed her the mortgage calculations I printed out.

"I guess you can afford it if you're putting down $200,000... wait a minute... where the hell are you getting' $200,000 from?"

"Mind your fuckin' business!" I laughed.

"Ooohhhh.... OOohhhkkkaaayyy – it's like that now?" she laughed.

"Here's what it looks like on the inside," I said as I showed her the flyer.

"Oh my God Trenice – it's beautiful!" she yelled when she saw the flyer.

"Yes it is...," I sighed.

"You better snatch this up quick."

"Oh I will – don't worry," I laughed.

"You've already made up your mind haven't you?"

"Yup."

"I see why you wanted to come over here and use my phone," she laughed.

"I really just wanted to get outta the house Ma," I sighed.

"I know you wanna get outta Ma's house," she laughed.

"No Ma – that's not it – ever since last week Grandma's been acting different," I sighed.

"Whataya mean different?"

"I think she's mad 'cause all the shit that went down," I sighed.

"Oh well – scratch your ass and git glad," she laughed.

"Damn Ma."

"Oh Trenice please – it's not that serious – if she's mad at you 'cause you told me she knew all along what happened – so what," she said as she finished her coffee.

"I guess...," I sighed.

"Trenice?"

"Yes?"

"Are you sorry you told me?"

"Hell no!"

"Alright then."

"I just wish Grandma wasn't mad at me," I sighed.

"Trenice?"

"Yes?"

"Scratch your ass and git glad," she laughed.

"You're right Ma," I sighed.

"Well if I'm right then stop feelin' sorry for yourself – let's go show Jordan your new home!" she yelled as she jumped up, snatched me by the arm, and pulled me towards the door.

Tracy Wilson

"Sounds good to me," I said as I snatched up the papers, folded them, and put them in my pocket as we headed downstairs.

"Hey Claire, hey Trenice," Miss April said as we passed her in the hallway."

"Hey April," my mother said as we continued downstairs.

"Hi Miss April," I said as we headed out the building and down towards Jordan's job.

"This is a pleasant surprise," Jordan said as he kissed me hello. "What brings you here?"

"Lunch," my mother said as she snatched Jordan by the hand and headed towards the door...

"Aiight y'all – I guess I'm going to lunch!" Jordan laughed as we all headed out the door. "So where we headed?" Jordan laughed.

"Parkside Diner," my mother said.

"Okay then," Jordan said as we started walking towards the diner. "Everything ok?" Jordan asked as we continued walking...

"Everything's fine," I said as we walked up the steps and into the diner.

"Good afternoon – table for 3?" the hostess asked.

"Yes please," my mother said as we followed her to the table and sat down.

"I'll send the waitress right over – enjoy your lunch," the hostess said as she went back towards the entrance.

"What's going on Beautiful?" Jordan asked.

"You and Trenice have a date tonight!" my mother said as I pulled the papers out of my pocket and handed them to him.

248

"Ohhhh.... This is nice!" Jordan said as he looked at the pictures.

"Yes it is – the blue sectional will fit perfectly in your new living room," my mother said.

"Ya know... now that I look at it... you're right Miss Claire," Jordan laughed.

"You see Trenice printed out the mortgage calculator with all the figures," she laughed.

"Yes I did," Jordan laughed.

"I asked her where the hell y'all getting' $200,000 from and she told me to mind my fuckin' business," she laughed.

"Trenice!" Jordan yelled.

"Relax Jordan," my mother laughed. "I've been tellin' Trenice she needed to start tellin' people to mind their fuckin' business for so long when she said it to me it was actually quite funny," she laughed.

"Yes it was," I laughed.

"Besides, I know where you got the money from anyway," she laughed again.

"May I take your order?" the waitress interrupted.

"We haven't even had a chance to look at the menu yet," Jordan laughed.

"You don't need to look at the menu Jordan – we'll have three orders – chicken parmigiana with spaghetti – and 3 ice teas," my mother said.

"I'll be right back with your drinks," the waitress said as she left the table.

"So when shall I pick you up for our date?" Jordan asked.

"We'll meet you there tonight at 6:00 p.m.," my mother said before I got a chance to answer him.

"We?" I asked.

"Yes – you, me, and Vanessa," my mother laughed.

"Okay then," Jordan said as the waitress brought our ice teas and placed them on the table.

"So how do you like your new home?" my mother asked.

"Now I see where Trenice gets it from," Jordan laughed.

"No sense in beatin' around the bush," my mother laughed.

"So did you tell your grandmother?" Jordan asked.

"Hell no – she came straight to my house – she even called Vanessa from there," my mother laughed.

"That's not like you Trenice – what's wrong?"

"Ma got a bug up her ass 'cause all the shit that happened last week – but she'll get over it," my mother laughed before I could answer the question.

"She has an attitude with you Trenice?" Jordan asked as the waitress brought our lunch and placed it on the table.

"Ma has an attitude with everybody," my mother laughed.

"Will there be anything else?" the waitress cut in.

"Just bring me the check," my mother said.

"Okay then," the waitress said as she walked away.

"I told my mother Grandma has a bug up her ass because of the way she talked to me this morning," I said as we ate.

"So how did she speak to you?" Jordan asked.

"She said she thought I'd be a pain in Vanessa's ass tryin' to get the hell out after what happened last week," I said.

"Damn... that was a little rough," Jordan said.

"I know. She heard me talkin' about this flyer but I told her it was about Poltergeist II," I laughed.

"Oh I see," Jordan laughed.

"So I told her I thought that was a good idea and I'd give Vanessa a call later today and she told me if I'd stop printing out my emails and go pick up the damn phone I just might get outta her house sooner," I said.

"Damn ‑ she really is mad," my mother laughed.

"Oh well... too bad," Jordan laughed.

"See Trenice – I told you," my mother said.

"Yea... I guess...," I said.

"I wouldn't worry about it Beautiful," Jordan said.

"Easy for you to say," I said.

"Look at the bright side Beautiful," Jordan said as he kissed me with saucy lips... "We'll be together, you and your mother are closer, and this'll all be in the past," he said as he finished his spaghetti, and then kissed me again.

"I knew you were good for Trenice," my mother said as she raised her glass.

"To us," Jordan said as we toasted and sipped our ice tea.

"Here's your check – thank you for choosing Parkside," the waitress said as she left the check on the table and went back towards the register.

"I'll get that," Jordan said as he tried to take the check.

"Who did she leave the check with?" my mother asked.

"You Miss Claire," Jordan said.

"Take your hands off the check and put them where they belong then," my mother laughed as she got up from the table and went to pay the check.

"Commere Beautiful," Jordan said as he pulled me into a passionate kiss.

"I love to see a man follow instructions," my mother laughed as she came back to the table, left the tip, and we all left the diner.

"Thanks for lunch Miss Claire," Jordan said as we started walking back towards his job.

"My pleasure – consider it a pre-celebration to the celebration," my mother said.

"You already have us moved in don't you?" Jordan asked.

"Actually, Trenice already had you moved in before she came to the house," my mother laughed.

"Oh she told you that?"

"She didn't have to – I know my daughter," she laughed. "Ok Trenice – I'm gonna leave you here with Jordan – I gotta few stops to make – if I don't see you back at the house I'll see you later tonight," she said as she crossed the street and went through the square.

"You are more like your mother every day Beautiful," Jordan said as we sat down on the bench.

"Thank you," I laughed. "Aren't you going back to work?"

"In a minute... but we need to talk first."

"We do?"

"Yes... about this condo..."

"You don't like it?"

"I love it…"

"I knew you would!" I yelled as I grabbed him into a hug…"

"I don't think we can afford it Beautiful," he said with his head down."

"Of course we can," I said as I took his hand.

"I looked at the figures you printed out – you used the mortgage calculator based on a $200,000 down payment and the remaining balance to be paid over 30 years plus maintenance – it'll be a little tight."

"Actually I just did that for my mom – I was hoping we wouldn't have a mortgage at all."

"Trenice that'll take just about all the money we have – you really wanna do that?"

"I was thinking about it."

"We won't have anything left – we'll be sleeping on the floor," Jordan laughed.

"No we won't."

"What'll be left after we pay $321,000, then buy furniture?" he laughed.

"We'll have money left."

"Oh boy… what are you up to now Trenice?"

"Well when I talked to Vanessa she said the property hadn't been on the the market that long but the seller was anxious to sell."

"He might be anxious to sell, but we won't be able to talk him down – 600 North Broadway is a nice building – people are probably waiting to buy a condo in there."

"That's why we have to move quickly – and we can give him the cash so he won't have to wait for a bank to approve our mortgage and we won't have to worry about board approval."

"You're right – but what makes you so sure he'll take our offer and not wait until someone else comes along to meet his asking price? Especially since it's a hot property?"

"I'm willing to take that chance – besides, even if we have to meet his price – we can do that and we'll still have some money left."

"We could end up spending all the money we have Trenice."

"Look at it this way – if we give him his asking price and we furnish it the way we want it – worst case scenario – we'll have the home we want with no mortgage – we may only have about $50,000 left in the bank but we'll be able to do this without borrowing from our pension or the credit union."

"You have a point there."

"So we'll do it?"

"You really want this don't you?"

"Yea...," I sighed.

"Good thing we got great deals on those cruises," he laughed as he kissed me.

"I'll see you tonight – I love you!" I yelled as I jumped up off the bench and made a beeline towards my mother's house.

Chapter 53

"Ma you ready?"

"Yea Trenice – hang on a second," she said as we opened the door.

"I'm so excited!" I yelled.

"I know – I am too," she laughed as we started downstairs.

"Where y'all headed?" Miss April asked as we passed her in the hallway.

"We're on our way to meet Jordan – we'll see ya later," I said as we went downstairs and outside.

"Hi Vanessa," I said as we got in the car. "This is my mother, Claire."

"Nice to finally meet you Claire. Is Jordan coming Trenice?"

"He's meeting us there," my mother said.

"Okay then," she said as we headed up North Broadway.

"There's Jordan waiting outside," Vanessa said as we drove up to the front of the building.

"Hey Beautiful," he said as he kissed me hello.

"Hi Jordan – nice to see you again," Vanessa said as she got out the car.

"Hello Vanessa, Hello Miss Claire," Jordan said

"Well let's go inside," my mother said.

"We will – but I'd like to show you around first," Vanessa laughed.

"Welcome to Hillcroft Towers – I'm Carl," the doorman said as he extended his hand to Vanessa's.

"Nice to meet you Carl – I'm Vanessa from Weichert Realtors and this is Jordan, Trenice, and Claire," she said as we followed her towards the main entrance.

"We've been expecting you," Carl said as we continued towards the main entrance. "As you can see, the grounds are meticulously maintained," he said as we looked around. "We have a 24 hour concierge desk, a business center, and a gym on the first floor," he said as we followed him through the glass doors into the marble lobby, and then went into the elevator.

"This certainly is a beautiful building," my mother said as we went up to the 13th floor. "I can't wait to sit out on the terrace with you and have my coffee...," she sighed. Vanessa looked at us and smiled.

"This way please," Carl said as we went down the hall to the last door on the right.

"Oh I like this already," Jordan said when we got to the end of the hall. "We're facing the river and we don't have anyone over our heads," he said as we went inside.

"Take your time – just close the door on your way out," Carl said as he left us in the condo.

"So what do you think?" Vanessa asked.

"I think I'll go out on the terrace," my mother laughed.

"Okay – we'll start with the kitchen and meet you out there," I said as I pulled Jordan through the living room, dining room, and into the kitchen.

"Nothing beats an updated kitchen," Jordan said as we looked at the new appliances, new cabinets, and marble countertops.

"It really is beautiful – and he just had the dishwasher put in," Vanessa said.

"Let's check out the ½ bath," I said as we went back through the living room to the bathroom.

"Very nice," Jordan said as we looked in.

"I love the pedestal sink, the marble floor, and the shower with the glass doors," I said.

"The owner really kept this place nice – the hardwood floors are new too," Vanessa said as my mother passed us on our way down the hall to the bedrooms.

"These bedrooms are huge – and look at the closet space we have honey," I said as Jordan and Vanessa followed me.

"Well, we know your clothes will fit," Jordan laughed.

"Let me show you the laundry closet before you see the master bedroom," Vanessa said as my mother passed us again.

"I think you made a mistake Vanessa," I laughed.

"Is this too small for you?" she asked.

"It is too small – hell no – it's so big we could fit a bed and a dresser in here!" I laughed.

"Yes, you do have plenty of room to do your laundry, separate it, and fold it," she laughed.

"It's like we have our own little mini-mat," Jordan laughed.

"Shall we go to the master bedroom now?" she asked.

"Not yet – I wanna check out the deck first, I said as she followed us out onto the deck.

"Oh my God – it's beautiful!" Jordan and I said in unison as we stood there observing the purple sunset.

"I knew you'd love it," she said as my mother sat there gazing out over the deck.

"I'll sit down here with your mother while you two go check out the master bedroom," she said as she joined my mother at the table.

"Okay Vanessa – we'll be right back," I said as we went through the living room and down the hall towards the master bedroom.

"I'm just waiting for them to make the offer," Vanessa laughed.

"I guess you know them pretty well huh?" my mother laughed.

"This place is perfect the them – I just hope they can get a mortgage – you know how tough banks can be – especially for first time home buyers – they have good credit but this is kinda pricey – they'll need a good down payment – even with their good credit," she said.

"Vanessa, you have nothing to worry about," my mother laughed.

"Ohhh... okay... thanks for the heads up – but they'll have to meet the asking price – this owner won't settle for anything less..."

"Why the hell should he?" my mother laughed. "All they have to do is move in!"

"You're right," Vanessa laughed.

Meanwhile... down the hall in the master bedroom...

"Oh my God!" Jordan and I exclaimed as we walked in.

"We have our own private suite Beautiful," Jordan said as he picked me up, spun me around, and fell back onto the bed with me.

"Well... unless you wanna put on a private show for Vanessa and my mother, we better get up," I laughed.

"You're right," he laughed as he pulled me up.

"I wonder if he'll let us keep the carpet?" I said as we walked across the plush teal carpet and into the walk-in closet.

"Hell – this is practically a room within a room!" he laughed.

"Yes it is...," I sighed.

"On to the piece de resistance," he said as he took me by the hand into the master bathroom.

"Oh my God – it's beautiful!" I whispered as we looked around at the marble floor, separate shower with glass doors, double porcelain sinks, lighted mirrors, marble vanity top, and the Jacuzzi with a curved sliding glass door and a glass wall with a clear view back into the bedroom.

"He certainly has exquisite taste," Jordan said as he took me by the hand, opened the curved sliding glass door, led me into the Jacuzzi, and closed the curved sliding glass door behind us. We stood in the Jacuzzi holding each other as we looked through the glass wall into the bedroom. "We're gonna make some beautiful memories here Beautiful," he said as he picked up my face and kissed me gently.

"Yes we will," I said as I kissed him back. We continued kissing for what seemed like an eternity until we were interrupted...

"I knew we'd find you two in here," my mother laughed as she slid the curved sliding door to the Jacuzzi open.

"So you'll take it?" Vanessa asked.

"We'll take it," we answered in unison as we followed Vanessa and my mother down the hall, out the door, and down the hall, arm in arm, to the elevator. We didn't say anything in the elevator but our smiles said it for us as Vanessa and my mother looked at us and at each other.

"Good night Carl," Vanessa said as we left the building."

"Good night Vanessa, good night Claire – welcome to Hillcroft Towers Jordan & Trenice," he said as we drove away.

Excerpt from:

How Far Are You Willing To Go? (Rated PG) – Part 2

"I just wanted everything to be perfect," I cried as he stroked my hair.

"Everything is perfect," he said as he picked up my face and kissed me. "We're here. Together. I don't give a damn about the food," he said as he pulled my face to his and kissed me passionately. "I just want to be with you."

"I wanna be with you too," I whispered as I started crying again.

"Now that's more like it," he said as he started to lift up my skirt. "Trenice what the hell is this on your skirt? Is this blood?"